DIZCHORD

ATLANTA'S GUARDIAN ANGEL OF MUSIC

ISSUE #1

Light Novel Edition

C. S. Johnson

Once Upon a Time in Atlanta …

Get the comic version on https://www.csjohnson.me

AUTHOR'S AFFILIATE LINK NOTICE:

Some links in this book are affiliate links from Amazon, Draft2Digital, and PublishingCenterUSA. They will be designated at the time of their writing. I would not be an affiliate of these companies if I didn't like or use their products and/or services. I do get some money if you click on them and/or sign up with them, but it's minimal. Again, it's not worth it if I didn't like them enough to do it in the first place, and really, I almost didn't do it anyway.

AUTHOR'S NOTE:

This book is not meant to be about anyone in particular and it is a product purely of my own imagination—but one of the most depressing points about writing this story is realizing how plausible it is, and how likely it is that it's happening already. So, for the record, given the content, if the worst happens, I didn't kill myself.

AUTHOR'S NOTE ABOUT *DIZCHORD*

Dear Reader,

Dizchord is a serial, episodic work of fiction. Set in quasi-contemporary Atlanta, GA, this series is part superhero fiction, part crime thriller, part family drama, and part political spy fiction. It is meant to be read in its original comic form, but as a novelist first and a comic book writer second, I understand the allure of a good book.

This book is a novelization of Issue #1. It hints at elements in the comics further down the line and in some cases adds to the story, but it contains the full story from the comic. I hope you'll enjoy seeing how this adaptation resonates with the heart of my story, and my own heart as well.

Wishing You All the Best,

Until We Meet Again,

C. S. JOHNSON

<u>ACKNOWLEDGEMENTS</u>

This book is dedicated to my fabulous donors and pledgers on Issue #1's Kickstarter. Even though the campaign failed to launch, I am truly thankful for your support and I hope that despite all my uncertain fumblings and various other shortcomings, I can reciprocate your kindness, and God willing, I will be able to prove myself a good investment in your future entertainment choices.

My Wonderful Kickstarter Pledgers:

Theo Kings
Chris Trixx Rand
Terri Rand
Jeremy Carl Reynolds
Jon Del Arroz
Fiannawolf
Hanz G. Sanchaz
Jon
Sol
Stephen Dawkins
SilverlineComics
Diggz
Mark
Pavlos C.
John F. Trent
Spencer Baculi
Christina
Klikke Siestel
Deborah O'Connell
Winter
Rachael Kraft

Leon Alston
Angela R. Watts
hairman
Jarrod Cline
Sabrina Zielinski (Mama Z)
Leon Idol
Connie Hendryx
W D Smith
Project 13
Douglas Wise
Paul Leone
Ron Brooks
Kerstin
Michael
CultClassicCage
Zekk
John Averette
Alan Blank
FedStarSaber
The Creative Fund by Backerkit

MY KO-FI SUPPORTERS

My Ko-Fi supporters support me outside of my work with tips and monthly financial donations. I am constantly humbled by their thoughtfulness, and I am so grateful for each moment of their time they've given me and my work.

Cathy H.
Laura P.
Terri R.
Gay D.
Andrea S.
Anne-Marie S.
Crystal M.
Jacob A.
Bonnie R.
Bryn S.
Beth C.
Donna S.
Daniel S.
Marty H.
Christian S.
David W.
Jerilyn B.
Christian S.
Marty H.
Daniel W.
G. E.
Stephen D.
Melinda M.
Jeremy R.
Krissy F.

CHAPTER ONE

* ♪ *

ONCE UPON A TIME IN ATLANTA …

Silence is always the heaviest sound among the city streets.

Atlanta was a city born of hope and opportunity, before it was reborn out of sheer persistence. The song it plays carries the past as it merges with the present. As I walk, I can feel the generations past: chants from its natives, the hymns from the pilgrims, drum beats from its colonists, and gospel songs of former slaves—all of them combine with modern day's non-stop rock, hip-hop, R&B, and more, all singing out the city's music.

Its energy is both potent and airy, pervasive and evasive, ebbing and flowing with and around each human soul—something felt but never seen, something tangible but never caught.

And so, where there's silence, there's suspect.

Especially at night.

And no one knows this better than me, Stephen Kibwaa—although I'm known to the public as Dizchord, Atlanta's very own guardian angel.

At least, that's how I see it; I like it better than 'resident superhero,' or 'vigilante.'

As the sun finally bows down to the power of the night, I straighten my shoulders.

It's time.

My heart pulses with a new beat as I pull my hood over my head. I press my mask more firmly on my face, and then I reach behind me, checking my bo staff batons; both have a special coupler on one end that lets it combine into one, but for now, they're separated and secure on my back. My suit is both shadow and light against the night; my gloves are secure, and my feet are light as I run.

I grimace, and then smile; I still hate running, but I've gotten better at it over the years.

It's not my first mission, but I'm still anxious.

When you're young, going out and fighting crime is a worthy dream; in reality, playing vigilante is a nightmare, especially with human traffickers.

The training was hard on my body, but brutal on my heart.

Painful memories slice through my concentration, and the old anger and the cry for blood stir to life; the temptation for vengeance is never far behind the call for justice.

My steps falter ever so slightly; but a moment later, remembering my training, I take a deep breath and push forward even faster.

As I run, I center myself, I say a silent prayer; I think of how far I've come—despite my pain, despite my losses, despite my fears.

I think of all the people who've helped me to get to this point.

And then I think of all the people who I can help, and I keep on keeping on.

Soon enough, I turn the corner and duck down into an alleyway. I'm just up from West End; just off to the side, I can see Atlanta's bright skyline. Above me, the full moon's peeking through the clouds, making the light-polluted skies muted and soft.

Seeing the signs along the street, I know I'm almost there. Gabe said he'd heard rumors of a drop-off, and I know I can count on him.

Only moments before, I could hear the late-night, downtown chit-chatter of vibrant life in the distance. Now, the silence is as thick as it is malevolent. It's times like this, I'm grateful for my suit; I designed it to deal with various weather concerns, among other things.

West End is slowly getting gentrified, but that's part of the reason it's the perfect cover for human traffickers. It was once a big transportation hub, but over the years of city growth, corrupt politics, and big business investments, the older buildings here are still echoes of the past. The cement sidewalks and building walls have their share of cracks; windows here and there are cracked and dirty, and the surrounding plant life is attempting to make a comeback.

Except where business is booming.

I notice the streets have been cleared at the intersection by an old warehouse and the old trolley station. The building is dark, but the surrounding wiring is new, and everything is silent.

Until I hear it.

There it is.

There's a chime in the air that only I can hear, and it's one I've easily come to recognize.

Despite the terrible situation and the undesirable setting, I can't stop myself from grinning.

This is my superpower.

This is my gift.

Ever since the day of my dad's funeral, I've been able to hear the song inside of each individual soul.

No one else can hear it, no one else can see it. None of my counselors or my therapists believed me when I told them, or even when I tried to prove it to them. It didn't take me long to stop expecting them to have answers for me.

The chime cries out again, stronger this time, and I force myself back to the present.

I clasp my hands together and cock my ear toward the source of the mystical music. An instant later, my palms light up with a mysterious and wonderful glow; it's a sustaining but scorching sensation, one I am both burdened and blessed with.

A small string of golden light appears, flickering in out of the darkness, twisting into a bar of musical notes. Each note twinkles as it dances around my palms, leading me towards its source. I follow its lead, the light like a lamp for my feet.

Just ahead of me, a ladder is hanging off an older building—a decaying fire exit. I decide to take the high route. It's dark enough I'll be able to blend into the night without a problem.

As I move upward, the music around me grows stronger.

It's the song of a soul, and this soul in particular is crying out with pure suffering, loneliness, and fear—but it also has a small spark of hope.

The second my feet hit the roof ledge, I narrow my eyes in angry recognition.

A child. This song is belongs to a child!

I can picture the boy now, squeezed into a corner of a large trailer, his teeth chattering from fear as he rubs his hands to find any warmth. He's hungry and lonely; he aches from the long drive. His heart is crying out as he misses his mother; and while he's suffering, he's still trying not to cry like the other kids around him.

Pure, righteous rage flows through my blood, and my hands begin to shake.

All this pain in the world, and there's someone out there determined to make it worse by sacrificing children for a payday.

I slowly unclench my fists.

Why am I so surprised? I shouldn't be.

According to Gabe's sources, that is exactly what is supposed to happen tonight. A delivery of fresh cargo is expected at the West End hub—and Conductor Marxman himself is supposed to be overseeing this shipment.

Marxman.

At the thought of the man who'd murdered my father, my mind instinctively conjures up my own malevolent wishes. I have to breathe and calm down again to channel my longstanding fury.

The little boy's soul song softly continues. I've been reminded countless times by Father Mike that the pains of my past cannot be fixed by vengeance, and that I will have to wait for the justice that comes with time and faith. In the meantime, I am called to protect others in the present, so the future might be brighter.

As I stand there, in the dark, I hate the reminder, but I know I need it, too.

There is more than my own pain to see to tonight, I tell myself.

Focus.

"Hold on," I whisper. The notes in front of me twinkle again, as if to carry my message back to the boy. I desperately want to believe he can feel my determination to save him and the others, despite the distance between us. "I'm on my way."

♩

At first, when I started going after the various groups of human traffickers, I didn't face the coyotes directly. I'd go in and upset the sale, sneak in half-way through the delivery, or catch the kidnappers off guard.

Once, I smuggled a handful of foreign women out of a construction truck without the driver discovering me; another time, I found a few kids hiding away in the sewers; and last time, I stopped a full eighteen-wheeler after using a knife on their tires.

I still have to laugh at that one—Atlanta traffic is notoriously awful, and the backed-up lanes on I-85 were legendary. Even the city news had to pick up the story, even if it was quickly shuffled through the programming and buried beneath some celebrity divorce and the rising amount of malaria cases in the city.

Now, I do things a little differently.

I prefer going in swift and hard, taking out the bad guys, getting the kids and other victims, and moving them out before anyone notices they are missing.

But eventually, I did have to face my enemies.

And I was ready for them.

Thanks to my dad and Sensei Shawn, I've been taught well, in self-defense—jujitsu, karate, bo staff, and more—and I have a secret weapon in my arsenal.

My power.

The music of each life brims over with dreams and memories, hopes and fears, thoughts and feelings. The more I focus, the more I can pull out images from their mind, and the more I can manipulate it myself.

It's dangerous, and there's always a price to pay when men make-believe that they're God. I'm no exception to that rule. It's only by His grace I've been able to hold firm against that temptation, and it's only by His power I'm here doing this at all.

But I do like using it to help others; it's a joy and privilege to offer comfort to the sad, to help someone feel loved when they're lonely, and to give them something to laugh at when nothing seems right.

I also enjoy using it on the villains who deserve to know the depths of their own self-hatred.

It wasn't long after I started using my power that Atlanta came to know me as "Dizchord." I think they thought it was cool, and as a musician myself, I couldn't disapprove of it.

"Come on." A man's voice interrupts my thoughts as his bulky frame slinks out of the shadows below me. I look down, and I see it; there's a large, dirty eighteen-wheeler ready to go under a dusky streetlight. I don't have to open it to know there are children inside; I can feel their fear and hear their sniffles.

Glancing down, I see the outline of a hat on a man's head flapping slightly in the breeze as he moves. He's thick around the middle, and it sounds like he's eating something as he speaks. "All's I'm saying is that we can get a better price—"

"No one breaks their deals with Conductor Marx," another man says with a scoff. I lean over the building's ledge, watching him as he spits onto the sidewalk. His face is hidden in the shadows just like his friend, but I see he has extra help from his beard. "He's not known as 'The Marxman,' for nothing, you know. He's always got his gun on him."

My hands curl into fist.

Marxman. He is coming tonight. He'll be here—if he's not already.

A taller man in a suit steps out to meet the others; I recognize him briefly as Bernard Marcello. He's been on the Marxman's roster for years, one of his highest-ranking henchmen. I've seen him hang back at some of the other drop-offs and hand-offs I've interrupted, although he's always managed to make his exit before the cops appear.

"What's this?" Bernard scoffs. "Someone's offered you a better price?"

"It's a competitive market," the first guy says with a wicked chuckle. "That's all I'm saying."

My anger is boiling, and I start to move down toward them as slowly as I can. There's a few ledges and windows off to the side that let me climb back down, and I take them.

By the time I reach the ground, I'm fired up, and ready to go.

That's when I hear *her* voice.

"I'd hate to tell my boss."

I stop in my tracks, caught off guard as I recognize it.

Kathleen.

I picture her in my mind before I can see her in the moonlight.

It's been years since our last meeting—Dad's funeral, but I still remember seeing her for the first time. That was back when I was invited to play at the Falcons game—when I was sixteen, almost ten years ago.

Kathleen McKinley was Dad's boss, one of his direct overseers and a case manager for ELEMENT's directors. He'd known her over the year he'd worked for ELEMENT. She'd always struck me as the diligent, dedicated public servant, and I remember thinking she was pretty enough and good enough with kids that she could've had a family of her own if she'd wanted one.

I shake my head, full of disgust.

There's blood on Kathleen's hands, and her cronies', too.

They've bought children for unspeakably evil pleasures of their clientele—and now I know for certain Kathleen was somehow involved in the death of my father.

My own inner symphony pulsates with new, vengeful power; I let it flow, willing it to help me subdue my enemies with all of my strength.

"No need to worry about your boss," the second man tells Kathleen, pulling me out of my jarring cacophony. "We got his order right here, and we know it's his."

I take in a few more deep breaths, forcing myself to focus.

The boy's miserable inner music comes crying out to me again, and I'm almost grateful for his pain, since it makes me forget my own. It's a cowardly kind of courage, but it's still better than having none.

"Come on, let's get this finished up," Kathleen says. "Marxman wants this out, pronto. Thanks to Governor Hailey, the police are bogged down some, but it won't be long before they get back to their rounds. We'd better be out of here by then."

They start to move, and so do I.

It's time.

The trailer bed is hitched up and the thugs are nearly ready to go by the time I get down to the street. I figure I only have a few moments to do what needs to be done.

A larger plane takes off and heads directly north over me—probably the 11:45 to LAU.

They're right on time …

Over the years, I've gotten really good at keeping time in my head, although it helps knowing the flight schedules for Hartsfield-Jackson. If anyone gets curious as to why I'm interested in the planes, I tell them I'm thinking of joining the Air Force, like my dad did. But really, it's my way of tracking my time, even if I don't have a watch or a phone with me.

Even before I became known as Dizchord, it was too easy to track people using phones and other technology. So I've left my phone at home, turned off, letting everyone know I'm "studying" for the night.

Which reminds me, I have a test coming up …

I shove that thought into the back of my head as I hear a small whimper coming from the truck.

It's barely audible, just a flicker along the wind.

But it's enough to focus my fire, and as I keep my eyes on Kathleen, I decide it's time to make my appearance.

I press down my mask, pray a silent prayer for justice, and step out onto the sidewalk.

"What is that?" Kathleen asks, as I scrape my boots against the ground.

I know the exact moment when everyone sees me; the sound of the street goes thick with silence, and I smile as I feel their hearts begin to beat violently with fear.

The dull streetlight serves as a spotlight for me, and my audience is mesmerized with terror. The shocked expression on Kathleen's face is almost worth her betrayal—there's nothing like seeing justice arrive in real time.

The half-second passes, and Kathleen comes to her senses and whips out her gun.

"Who are you?" she demands, and the others quickly step forward to fight.

"Stop. We'll handle this," Bernard assures her bitterly as he pulls out his knife. "No need to draw the cops' attention with gunshots."

I don't bother to tell them the police are coming anyway, thanks to some well-timed anonymous tips I'd phoned in earlier; instead, I grab my batons and get to work.

There's nothing like the rush of battle. Bernard and his friend both have knives brandished as they rush at me, and I rush at them, but it's only a matter of seconds before I have Bernard in a headlock and the other guy is bleeding on the ground.

I let go of Bernard, punch in his nose and thrust my foot into his kneecap. He falls to the ground fast, and he's smart enough to roll away before his colleague takes his turn.

He rushes forward, and I lash out with a kick right in his face. He goes flying back, and I can't stop smirking as I think how proud Sensei Shawn would be; I'm getting much better with my kicks, and it's welcome to see the proof stamped on the face of a slaver.

Bernard has recovered enough to find another knife. I grab my current attacker, watching as Bernard slices his knife our way.

The blade lands smartly in the stomach of my attacker, and I do my best not to listen to his cries of pain.

I hate feeling sympathy for evildoers; I hate wishing they'd taken other jobs, made better decisions, and stood for higher ideals. The church believes in sin, and the fallen nature of man, and I've seen enough of it to believe Hell is a just punishment for those who enjoy and delight in the darkness sin has to offer. Its short-term pleasure comes at the cost of others, and the long-term collateral damage can echo through generations.

And don't I know that myself? My dad was killed by the Marxman, and I still feel the pain at his loss.

I slam my fist into Bernard's face, thrusting him to the ground.

His lips twitch in pain, before his eyes roll back into his head and he's out cold. Behind him, both of his accomplices are down—bleeding badly and unconscious, even though they're still alive.

I don't like the idea of killing others. Hell might be a just punishment for the bad guys, but I still hate the idea of sending anyone there myself.

"Who … are you?"

Kathleen's voice is a trembling whisper.

I look over at her, watching as she still has her gun pointed at me; her eyes are full of fear and anger and indecision, and I revel in knowing I'd been a successful, unpleasant surprise.

I recall Kathleen as I'd known her before, as my dad's boss, as one of the people who helped me, as someone who had once looked out for me … And then I think of how she's helped the Marxman kill my father, how she's destroyed my life, and the lives of countless others …

I don't want to send anyone to Hell … but …

There are exceptions to every rule.

I breathe again, letting the temptation slide through me. I feel its power; I yearn for its promise, even if I know it's an empty one.

My hands are shaking as I put my batons in their sheath.

Deep in my heart, I cry out for vengeance. I want to watch Kathleen and the others writhe in pain, I want to watch their blood run down theirs faces; I want to beat them mercilessly, all on behalf of all the lives they've destroyed …

But I know that won't bring Dad back.

And I know that Kathleen won't feel sorry for anything she's done, either—she'd only be sorry for getting caught.

"You … wouldn't hurt a woman, would you?" she asks softly. When I don't answer, and I only move closer, she cries out.

"Augh!" Kathleen falls down as she retreats. Her gun goes limp in her hand, and I take my opening.

I hold up my hand, focusing my power.

At once, I can see the oozing mess of her inner music—a woman who's known fear and loss her whole life, who seeks out money and power as a way to escape; someone who wants to be loved, even as she does the most evil and vile things possible.

I thrust her soul's song back at her, manipulating them to wrap around her. The notes fill her eyes and her whimpers grow increasingly loud.

"What have you done to me?" Her anguished yell fills the street.

"I've done nothing," I say, my tone bitter and angry. "I've only amplified the music of madness and discord inside your soul. You did the rest—and you would have done worse to others if I hadn't shown up to stop you … but then, I expect that of a dirty cop from ELEMENT. Especially one as dirty as you, Kathleen."

Tears slide down her face, and I suddenly recall how blasé and distracted she'd been at my dad's funeral ten years ago.

She slams her palms against her ears and crumbles to the ground. "He knows me?" she gasps, unable to fathom how I've used her own sins against her. "He knows me!"

Kathleen curls over in a fetal position as I force the large trailer open.

The sight before me is just as I'd figured; there are at least a dozen kids in the trailer. All of them flinch and shrink back from me as I stand in the shadows.

I look at them for a long moment, taking in each of their faces; several of them are foreigners' children, likely fresh from the coyotes' supply chain down near the Texas-Mexico border. Some of them look like they're children from the streets—one of the more disastrous consequences of homelessness in cities has been the neglected children, and opportunists have been quick to help "redistribute" them—while others still are clearly catering to a particular demand.

I reach up and push down my hood. "Don't be afraid," I tell them. "I'm here to help you, but if you wait just a little while longer, you can help others, too."

"What do you mean?" one little boy asks. He cautiously approaches me, and I recognize him at once; this was the same little boy whose song had cried out to me.

I kneel down in front of him. "I've been eager to meet Conductor Marx, the man who paid these goons to kidnap you and bring you here."

I pause for a moment; I don't want to say too much to the kids. They're still kids, after all, and they should have some right to remain innocent.

"Once I take care of the Conductor, Federal Agents will come, and they'll do their best to get you back to your families—or find you new ones."

"Really?" The little boy's eyes brim with tears as I nod. "Thank you. I want to go home. I want my mom!"

There's something about him that makes me look twice. "What about your dad?" I ask, suddenly curious. I don't have to wonder if my dad would've taken on the world to find me.

"He died shortly after I was born. I've never met him," the boy told me. "Not really, anyway. I don't remember him."

His matter-of-fact tone was heartbreaking to me; I miss my dad every day, and I can't imagine what it would be like to not have had him at all in my life.

"Maybe you'll meet him again one day," I say. "My dad died when I was younger, too, but I still see him from time to time."

"That's impossible," the boy says with a blatant defiance I recognized.

I'd once felt that way, too.

More of the children circle around me, and I can hear the police sirens in the distance as they approach us. I want to tell them to be brave, and take heart, and don't lose hope …

Just like Dad would've done for me.

So for now, I smile at them and huddle them closer. "Sometimes the impossible becomes the inevitable … "

DIZCHORD

CHAPTER TWO

* ♪ *

flashback to the past …

The first impossible thing I encountered in life was my father.

My dad was a man of faith first of all, and second he was a man who loved music.

He'd laugh as he'd tell me that was because he had nothing else; he'd grown up poor in Kenya, near the Ethiopian boarder, where the nuns from some of the missionary houses would feed him. His own father had died when he was younger, and his stepmother was constantly trying to poison him; eventually, he left their small community, looking for something more—something greater, as he'd said.

Dad would smile when he told me how he'd been walking across the dirt fields for three days when he heard the music pouring out from a small shack of a church. "Seeing it was a miracle," he told me once. "The music settled inside of my heart and never left. And when the nuns told me that God himself had called to me, I never hesitated to believe it. Music as beautiful as that wouldn't lie to me. It was like falling in love; I had nothing, and then I was swept away into everything."

Dad would tell me these stories when I was a teenager. Before, when I was just a little boy, I'd been eager to be just like my dad, and I would sit next to him while he practiced the piano. As I grew up, and I grew more surly, he pushed me to keep playing, and he would tell me these stories as I worked.

I mostly rolled my eyes or ignored him. I'm ashamed of that now, but I am happy that I still did my best. Once I was done, and Dad was happy with my efforts, I'd get to play my video games again. I'd think about that a lot while I played, even as Dad kept telling me about his life.

When Dad was older, around his mid-twenties or early thirties—it was hard to say exactly when, since he didn't really have a birth certificate or a family for his age reference—he learned English, and eventually immigrated to America, landing in New York City. He sometimes would get sad and wistful, recalling how he'd seen the Twin Towers standing tall in the foggy morning light.

He told me he came to the United States looking for opportunity, but he ended up falling in love all over again.

And not just with the country, which was beautiful and majestic, full of energy and hope and resilience.

It was then he met and fell in love with my mother, Linda.

"Your mother was a real angel," he'd tell me. "Hearing her sing was like hearing another call from God. I knew then that I was meant to be hers, and I set out to make her mine."

I almost smile, thinking of my younger self. "Gross, Dad," I'd muttered, practically gagging at the sentimentality of it all.

He'd only laugh at me. "You wouldn't be here if it weren't for all that gross stuff, son," he'd say, teasing me good-naturedly.

And he was right about that. A few years after Dad joined the Air Force, while he was working toward earning his Green Card.

I was born, and he became a father as well as an American citizen.

Dad remained in the Air Force for a time, before Mom got tired of moving around. Once he'd gotten in eight years on his military contract, he decided not to renew it, and we settled in Atlanta, Georgia, just a few miles away from the Dobbins Air Force base where he'd finished his last assignment. I'd just turned twelve the year he got out and became a cop for Atlanta's precinct.

By this time, Dad had come to love another thing about American culture: American football. He especially loved the Falcons, since he remembered seeing some back in Kenya. I guess it helped that he had a more sentimental reason for enjoying them, since the team didn't seem to win a lot. He kept talking about taking me to a game one day, and he would especially bring this up as I practiced my piano.

One day, I slammed my fingers down on the keys after a particularly frustrating scale.

"Come, now, Stephen," Dad said. "You'll get it. Good things take time to master. No one's an expert on anything right away."

"But I don't *want* to play the piano, Dad," I whined, crossing my arms across my chest. "I want to play video games and just be a bad-ass cop like you when I grow up."

"Watch your language, son," Dad said easily enough. "And that's fine, if you want to be a cop one day."

He came up beside me and played the first few keys. "But right now, I need you to put down your video games and keep practicing your piano."

"Aw, come on. You get to put down the bad guy! And I don't want to just play music. That's boring."

"Now, Stephen, tearing down the bad is easy; creating the good, now that's much harder. One day you'll learn how to fight; but right now, I need you to practice your music. If you're going to be a cop like me, you need something that will balance out all the ugliness with beauty."

"Mom!" I called out. "Tell Dad to give me a break, won't you?"

"You heard your father, Stephen," Mom called back to me. She appeared in the doorway as I sulked. "Put your games away and keep practicing. You'll thank your father for his persistence one day!"

Dad grinned at the sight of her; even as a kid, I knew it was a special thing to see how she made him smile so much.

"Well, you would be the one to know that, wouldn't you?" he asked Mom. He walked over to her and kissed her soundly. "Especially after all those times I asked you to marry me?"

"I think I remember thanking you for that several times, baby," Mom replied with a grin of her own.

She wrapped him into a hug and kissed him again, while I nearly gagged at their displays of affection.

Before I could get too disgusted, Dad came over and put his hand on my shoulder. It was his way of telling me to scoot over on the piano bench, and I half-willingly obliged. I always had more fun when Dad came and joined me.

He began playing along with me. I felt the warmth of his body as we played through the scale slowly, and I relaxed a little.

"There's something miraculous about music, Stephen," Dad told me. "Whether you know it or not. There's a middle C that doesn't change—it hasn't, and it won't ever … you need to keep a good balance to play well … there's a melody for every key, and a time for it to play … every discord can be used, or even resolved … and behind music's creation is a master composer. He is the one who pulls it all together in the end. Every soul, like every key, needs to be tuned and cared for … "

Out of the corner of my eye, I could see my mom watching him with such boundless love and admiration as Dad played the last little bit of the song.

I let out a reluctant sigh of admiration. "I don't know why you make me do this," I said. "I'll never play better than you. It's impossible."

"Sometimes the impossible becomes the inevitable, son … "

He leaned back as the music died, and I could only scowl. If anything, *he* was the impossible one.

* ♪ *

Dad never did let up on me learning to play the piano. And truth be told, I didn't mind it so much.

My mother was a music teacher, so a lot of people assumed I liked music because it was such an integral part of my life. And perhaps that was part of it—but there was more, too. Dad was right about music. There was something miraculous there, and there were days when I could feel it, even if I couldn't quite grasp it or explain it to other people.

Dad's said before there are some things about life that can only be experienced, that they can't be explained. He thought that about faith as well as music, and he took us to church on Sundays. Dad had grown up in Kenya, but he had been delivered from death and poverty and despair by the Ethiopian Orthodox Church, so we went to St. Elias's church in Atlanta.

I didn't always appreciate going to church; as I grew up, I grew frustrated by the rituals and the catechisms and the confessions and the sacraments. It seemed strange how it was at odds with a world that was full of logos, mottos, mantras, consumerism and collectivism by politics, race, and class. The world's secular religions were much easier for me to grasp for; it took work—hard, unpleasant work—for me to get better at my faith. I would sometimes just wish for God to prove to me that he was real—that I would see and feel and touch him, and I would know and never doubt again.

While I never really got an answer like that, I did feel some kind of soulful comfort in the songs and in the music there, and in my turbulent, tumultuous teenage years—even before Dad died—I did come to appreciate the faithful, steadfastness Christ and his church had to offer.

In some ways, I was surrounded by music my whole life.

I kept at it, even though it was hard and it took time away from my video games and having fun with my friends. I hated the thought of missing out, especially as I worried I was already going to miss out on enough because of Dad's job.

The year I turned fifteen, I started hating how Dad was a cop. A lot of people in my school hated cops at this time; there was a large push for cops to be defunded, and there was a lot of speculation that they were the real criminals.

Dad assured me that his precinct had a tight code of ethics, but he warned me that some trouble would always be unavoidable. And when Francesca Westlake-Hailey was elected Senator, she took this issue to task. My friends, classmates, teachers, and a lot of the celebrities filming near Atlanta all started parroting her talking points, and I didn't know what to believe.

I really only knew that I had to be more careful than ever not to let people provoke me into a fight. Plenty of my peers hated my dad for being a cop, and they enjoyed the chance to make my life miserable as some kind of petty payback.

But I knew Dad would be disappointed in me if I let them get to me. He encouraged me to keep my head held up high, to stand tall, and to be firm in my conviction. Even if people hated cops, it wasn't justice for them to take out their grief on me, or to let me suffer because of things that were outside my control.

But the day I pointed that out to a small crowd of bullies, I got beaten up pretty badly.

Several guys in my class held me down and beat me up; when Ms. Sanderson, tried to intervene, they told her that it was my fault, and I'd said that my dad would come and haul them off to jail, among other things.

"Is that true?" Ms. Sanderson asked, horrified. "Oh, Stephen, that's terrible!"

"I didn't say that!" I argued, as blood spurted out of my cut upper lip. "They're lying."

One of the bullies—the only one I recognized from my English class—Gabe Chapman, crossed his arms defiantly. "No, he is! And if I have to call my dad, I will!"

"Oh, Gabe, please," Ms. Sanderson begged. "You've already called him twice this semester."

Gabe smirked. "My dad never has any qualms about making sure I'm getting the education I deserve."

I narrowed my eyes at him. Gabe's dad was a big-time media reporter and his mom was a trust-fund baby with a lot of money. It was well-known that they used a lot of that money to buy favors with the schools and teachers, among others.

Ms. Sanderson looked at me with impatient pity. "This is something I don't need right now," she murmured. "We've got midterms coming up next month, and I need to get y'all ready for your exams. Let's just get to class and call it a day. Deal?"

"No," I scoffed, still bleeding.

The other boys laughed at me, and then they laughed harder as Ms. Sanderson sent me to the principal's office for "being disagreeable."

An hour later, Mom came and picked me up. She let me go to my room and lay down, promising me she would cook an extra-special dinner and that I could play my video games while I waited for Dad to get home.

"Mom, I can't keep going to school like this," I said, doing my best to keep the pain out of my voice.

She patted my hair. "I'm sorry, baby," she whispered, her eyes as sad as mine. "I'll talk to your father when he gets home."

"This isn't right!" I snapped.

"I know, Stephen, and that's why we need to talk about how to fix it," she said calmly.

She hugged me and held me for a long moment, and I let her; I squeezed her, letting all the furious rage inside of me channel through my embrace. She took it and held onto me firmly. There was a stark silence between us as we stood there.

"I love you," she said, as she finally loosened her grip on me.

It didn't seem like much, but it was enough. I knew I had her support.

Dad had been hesitant to let me learn how to fight for a long time, even with the bullies around. When I asked him why, he said he saw it as an extra layer of temptation—but there was more, too.

"What more?" I asked him that night, more than angry. "Do you think it's better for others to see me weak?"

"You don't understand, Stephen," he said, rubbing his head anxiously. "Once you learn to fight, and even how to defend yourself, you start to realize that life is a never-ending battle. You are still young, and I want you to have a good life … a happy life. I don't want you to pick up a burden you won't be able to put down."

"I already have one with you being a cop!" I shouted back, and Dad finally saw reason.

"Alright," he said. "Alright. I guess it's time … it's about time after all, I suppose … I'm not going to be able to hold off any longer. Not without compromising things."

I frowned. "What do you mean by that?"

He didn't answer me. Instead, he went out of my room for a moment. I glanced over my shoulder and watched for him, gazing on as he came back into the room. He had a pamphlet in his hand.

"I found it," Dad said. "It took me a few months, but I found your future mentor."

I gave him a quizzical look, but he just shook his head and shoved the pamphlet at me. "You'll be a great fighter one day, Stephen. But your progress will be painful."

"It'll be worth it, though," I insisted, grabbing at the pamphlet with eager hands.

Dad let me leaf through it on my own. "This is the Atlanta Martial Arts and Self-Defense Dojo," he said. "I've talked to a few people there, and I think it's time you start working with Sensei Shawn there. I've already paid for your lessons. He's promised to take care of you all the way up to your black belt for me, and I like the man. He's got a daughter your age, too, and they keep their dog at the dojo, so I think you'll like them. They're a good family, and they'll teach you to fight."

"Cool," I murmured, looking through the sections with the cool moves and the punching and the kicking. I sat there, soaking it up like it was a lifeline.

"It was a lot of money, but I know you'll need it."

Dad rarely, if ever, mentioned money to me, so I was surprised at his comment.

"You know, if it's too much money, you could save me a lot of trouble but just quitting the force," I said. "No one even likes cops in Atlanta anyway!"

"Bullies find excuses to fight with you," Dad said quietly. "My job is just one of them. It's not the problem, Stephen. And I like being a cop."

"Why?" I asked, amazed at his utter lack of self-awareness.

Dad thought about it for a moment and then he smiled. "Police are like the Falcons, son," he said.

"You mean they're losers?"

"No." He nudged my shoulders reproachfully, but he had a grin on his face. "They're protectors. I don't like the Atlanta Falcons because they're winners. God knows they don't win that much.

"But falcons are fighters, and they're not just fighting for the sake of fighting. They fight to defend their family and their freedom. Police are like that, too."

"Yeah, okay, sure," I mumbled.

"Maybe we'll get around to going to a game together one day, huh?" Dad smiled at me and ruffled my hair. "What do you think, son?"

He'd been promising me that we'd go together for a long time, but work always seemed to get in the way. Which was the other problem I had with his job, actually, and I made it a point to tell him that.

"I still want you to get another job, though," I said. "The others would stop picking on me if you weren't a cop."

Dad sighed, but he looked thoughtful. "We'll see, son. We'll see … "

*  *

For all Dad was reluctant to let me start fighting, he seemed to grow more certain he'd made the right choice in the following days. It helped that he was right about Sensei Shawn and his family; he was a good master, with kind words, biting humor, and a kind of world-weariness about him that I only recognize looking back on my earliest memories of him. He was a man who had seen trouble, fought with it, and walked away from it, although not unscathed.

The first time Dad introduced us, I still had a bit of a bloody lip, while the black and blue marks from around my eye had faded some. I didn't know what to say, other than offer him a tepid, "Hello, sir."

Sensei Shawn looked at me. I was relieved to see there was no pity in his gaze. "So, you must be Stephen. Your dad's spoken highly of you."

"Yes, sir," I repeated. "I'm here to learn how to fight."

"Not quite," he said. "Your dad's not paying me a small fortune to teach you how to be a fighter."

I looked at him, confused. "What do you mean?" I asked, as my anger began to boil over. "Can't you see I need to learn how to fight?"

"Any fool with fists can fight," Sensei Shawn said. "A fighter is someone who just wants to fight."

I narrowed my eyes, and he chuckled. I was pretty sure I wasn't going to like him, and I was about to say so, when he continued.

"It's my job to teach you to be a warrior," he said. "A warrior knows when to fight, not just how, and more importantly, he knows when he's won."

I muffled a frustrated groan, and Sensei Shawn seemed to take that as a sign to start.

He began to show me around the Dojo. He would introduce me to his daughter, Abby, who would eventually become one of my best friends, and their dog, Salamander, one of the sweetest and laziest dogs I'd ever met. He'd show me around the weights, the mats, and the weapons they used to train. He'd introduce me to the other instructors, some of the more advanced students, and the other employees. It was a small but efficient business, and while I couldn't wait to get started, Sensei Shawn insisted I ground myself there first.

Dad approved of this, and it wasn't long before I knew why he'd chosen him as my teacher. It was a few years later that I found out Dad had indeed paid Sensei Shawn that small fortune—ten years' worth of lessons, all in advance.

At the time, I didn't know this.

But I did like learning how to fight.

As Sensei Shawn and his family helped me grow into a competent fighter, Dad became more pleased to see my progress. Several times over the next few weeks, he told me repeatedly he was proud of me for my efforts. Over the next few weeks, I added karate and martial arts to my schedule, along with piano, church, school, and hanging out with my friends.

I told him it was fine, but we both knew that the real test would come when the bullies made their next move.

For a while I didn't notice the time passing, even if Dad's mood was growing a little darker each day. In addition to martial arts and self-defense, I still had piano, church, school, and hanging out with my friends.

But when I walked into school the day after Senator Westlake-Hailey called for the governor to step down after he vocally supported the cops following a deadly protest, they were waiting for me.

I was ready for them, too.

This time, Gabe was back as the lead goon, and he grabbed at my piano book.

"Hey!" I balked. Mrs. Nagy, the school's music department coordinator, had just given it to me so I could assist her with the Ugandan African Choir coming to America in the next few weeks. Mom had been thrilled at such an opportunity, and even I was glad to see something good come from all my practicing.

"What is it?" Gabe asked, looking through it. "Some kind of druggie drop off?"

I longed to ask him if he was confused because there weren't any pictures in the book, but I held back my words. Seeing an opening, I snatched it away from him.

"Just leave me alone," I muttered. "Unlike you, I don't need to pick on someone else to feel better about myself."

"Hey, Gabe's parents are rich," one of the other kids spoke up. "He doesn't feel bad."

"Sure, he doesn't," I snapped back. "That's why he's so great at making the world a better place, by beating me up."

Gabe cracked his knuckles. "It seems I've been too lenient on you of late. You've got an attitude problem now. Maybe the world will be a better place when you shut up."

He and his two friends flanked me, ready to fight.

But I was ready to do more than fight—I was ready to do battle.

And win.

Gabe threw the first punch, and I side-stepped it easily enough. My hands came up, and as his eyes widened in surprise, I took a fighting stance.

The others came behind him, and then I went on the attack.

I felt myself moving more than I told myself to move—everything became a blur as we battled out for our dignity, our pride, and our self-preservation.

My fists went out.

They closed around me.

My kicks landed hard.

I pushed their punches away.

They fell to the side.

I rolled to the ground.

And then, it was all over.

Gabe was on the floor, his nose broken, his eyes red from holding back his tears. His friends scrambled away, one of them fearfully laughing at Gabe, while the other shook his head.

"I told you I didn't wanna fight no more," I heard him mutter, as he stomped away with a small limp.

"What's going on here?" Ms. Sanderson came out into the hall and saw me standing over Gabe as he bled out. "Oh my God, what are you doing this time, Stephen?"

"Just getting along," I said, as I reached down and offered my hand to Gabe.

Gabe and I exchanged a glance; he was upset and angry with me, but as Ms. Sanderson bore down on us, he reluctantly took my hand and I pulled him up.

Gabe said nothing to me, and nothing to Ms. Sanderson, but she still sent me to the principal's office.

Mom and Dad had to attend a meeting, but in the end, they didn't punish me for fighting. Dad agreed it sounded like I had no choice but to stand up for myself, especially since the school had records of Gabe and his cronies picking on me. Later that night, I heard Mom ask Dad to look into getting a lawyer for me since the school didn't punish Gabe, but Dad said no.

"Why not?" Mom asked, clearly furious. "If I worked there, I would have been written up for negligence. That teacher and the principal deserve to be reprimanded."

"You might not work there, but you do work in the same district," Dad reminded her. "No need for them to think we're all troublemakers here."

"We might as well be," Mom snapped back. "They don't like you being a cop any more than Stephen does."

"Stephen is young," Dad reminded her. "One day, he'll know the full cost that comes with protecting other people, and the sacrifice that comes for standing up for what's right, and then he'll understand. For now, I'm happy he knows how to end a fight, and seemingly graciously, too. That's far more admirable than those who hate me simply because I'm a policeman."

Mom and Dad continued to talk; she was combative and eager for blood. As I listened, Dad let her work through her frustration, and he assured her my lessons at the dojo would do wonders for me for years to come.

I went to bed that night with a small smile on my face.

I had earned Dad's approval. And while he was still on Atlanta's police force, I could take care of myself.

The next several weeks seemed to pass in the blink of an eye. Gabe not only left me alone, but thanks to the rumors of how I'd demolished him and his flank of friends, he'd been cut off by high school society. He was the butt of a joke, and even as he tried to buy back his friends' love with his dad's money and his mother's connections, nothing seemed to work.

I didn't interact with him much, but when we approached each other in the hall, he would look me in the eye and then look away, as if he was ashamed.

Whether he was ashamed of himself, or me, I couldn't say.

I didn't think anything of it.

But a couple of days later, I was at my locker, grabbing my books and getting ready to go home, and as I shut my locker and did a double-take.

Gabe was standing there, waiting for me.

"What do you want?" I asked, suspicious.

He scowled, but he didn't step back. Instead, he held out his hand. "I'd like a truce," he said. "What do you say? Friends?"

I looked him over and felt disgust at the sympathy I felt. His nose was now just ever so slightly crooked from our battle, and without his friends to flank him, he looked a lot shorter and smaller than I remembered. I was tempted to ask him why he wanted to be friends with me, but I already knew the answer: he was lonely, and alone, and he'd been outcast from his social caste because of fighting with me.

"Fine," I said, as we shook on it. I didn't want to be enemies anyway.

He seemed relieved. "Fine. See you later, then."

He turned and left, and that was that. It wasn't much, but over the next several years, I came to appreciate Gabe a lot more, and we did officially become friends at some point, even if I can't remember the exact moment.

I went home that day feeling better than ever. It was nice to win a fight against a bully, but it was even nicer that I'd managed to turn my enemy into a friend.

I knew Dad would be proud of me.

I mostly forgot about it all until later, though, as I came in and saw Dad was home.

"Good news, Stephen!" he said, surprising me with a big hug. "I got a new job!"

"Oh, honey, that's wonderful," Mom called out from the other room.

"You did?" I asked, beyond surprised. The way Dad loved his job, and his friends on the force, I would've thought the world would split in two before he quit.

"Yes," he said. "I was recruited personally by the director of a new task force the federal government is putting together."

"Oh." My hopes deflated. "So now you're a super-cop?"

Dad only laughed, and Mom was smiling, too, as she walked into the room. From the way she held her phone, I knew she was talking to my Gram.

Mom glanced over at Dad. "Mama says she's proud of you, and she'll be even more proud of you once she knows how much you make and what benefits you're getting." Mom paused as my grandmother shouted at her over the phone, and then added, "Assuming you're getting more money and better benefits, that is."

Dad grinned. "You can tell Jada not to worry, as usual. The job comes with a lot of perks as well as benefits, too—fifteen percent pay raise, life insurance, and even some special assignments."

Mom smiled as Gram started whooping and shouting on the phone. I could hear her cheering, saying she expected Christmas to be particularly bright this year, and despite my reservations, I let out a cheer, too.

I'd been waiting for Dad to get a new job for so long, I hadn't really believed he would. True, it was still in law enforcement, but at least the people at school would find a new reason to mock me.

I was about to ask Dad if his new job meant I could get a new game system when Mom hung up the phone.

"Ben won't like it. He didn't take the news too hard, did he?" Mom asked as she hugged Dad.

For the first time, Dad's enthusiasm waned, and I got a sinking feeling in my stomach. As if sensing my doubt, Dad glanced over at me, and then resumed his joyful posture. "Ben's my best friend. He'll understand."

We all knew he was lying.

Ben Richards was the one who'd hired Dad on the force, all those years ago; he was my dad's best friend, even though Ben seemed more like a surrogate father to my dad. To me, it made sense, even though Ben was an older white guy, and my dad was an African immigrant; Ben had a son only a little younger than my dad, even though I'd never met him, and he had a couple of daughters as well. It only seemed to make sense he would feel like a father since he was already one; and for his part, Dad had been abandoned and orphaned at a young age, so he readily accepted this dynamic.

As for me, despite the backlash I got from school for having a cop in the family, I knew Ben had been there for my family more often than I could count, and he was quite passionate to make Atlanta a safe city. Like my dad, he'd been a military man, and even after years of dealing with political red tape, unrelenting bureaucracy, bitter disillusionment, he still showed up and worked hard. As I grew up, later on I would realize things hadn't been any easier for him; Ben had been passed over for several promotions and he was regularly called in for overtime.

"Maybe Mr. Ben can go with you," I suggested, but Dad shook his head.

"He'll never give up Precinct 1," Dad said with a sad smile. "He'll work himself to death, or he'll die on the job."

"Honey." Mom gave him a sideways warning glance.

Dad shrugged. "Stephen knows Ben well; he knows I'm only saying the truth."

We all went quiet for a moment, and then Dad cleared his throat. "So, my official title will be as a Special Agent, working with ELEMENT, a new organization that's backed by the government."

"ELEMENT?" I asked. "Sounds weird."

"It stands for an 'Elite League of Extraordinary Members Eliminating National Trafficking,'" Dad explained. "It may sound weird, but that's part of it. It's designed to go after child and human traffickers. So I think Ben will at least understand why I took the job. He'd never stop me from protecting others, especially kids."

"You might even make his job a little easier, with federal backing," Mom suggested as she gave Dad another hug.

"Yeah, that might be true," Dad agreed. "But he'll still be sad without me around. He'll miss ordering me around."

"He even does that when he visits us," I said with a scoff. "He probably won't stop."

"True enough." Dad tossed me his badge. "I didn't tell you the best part, Stephen. I'll be getting some special assignments, including some football games! So, we'll get to go see the Falcons play, courtesy of my new job. Isn't that wonderful?"

I gave him a skeptical look. "You'll still be working."

"That's nothing," he said. "We'll still be together, right? I'm keeping my promise to you."

Dad seemed happy, so I let it go.

I ran my hands over his badge. It was small but solid, and it shone brightly under the light.

Excitement started to take hold of me again. Dad's badge was bright and shiny, and perhaps the future was, too.

Or so I thought.

But then, how could I know Dad's new job would ruin everything?

* ♪ *

Life changed slowly at first—and then all at once.

In the beginning, I was caught up in everything, everything that came with the whirlwind of change.

ELEMENT paid for my family to move down further into Midtown. While it was only a few blocks away, it was a real step up from our current apartment; the new condo had an extra bedroom, a large kitchen and dining room, and even a balcony.

Gabe's friendship, as much as it seemed to be more of a penance to him than anything else, gradually allowed me to be accepted and left alone by our peers. I wasn't bullied any longer, and I was even able to get along with many of the people who'd previously avoided me. Word of my dad's job and my fighting skills also helped secure my new status quo. I went from a nobody to pick on to a somebody; and with that came a certain air of mystery and respect.

I didn't notice the downsides of Dad's new job for a long time. But slowly, I did notice there was a new pattern emerging; Dad was a lot more distracted, a lot more contemplative, and a lot more … cautious about the future. He started talking about making sure Mom and I would be alright if something happened to him; he would run off to church, sometimes in the middle of the night, to go pray with Father Mike, our priest; and then he would just seem so much more … hopeless.

Initially, I wrote it off, blaming the nature of his work. It was police work, and police work that dealt with saving children from kidnappers and people who would drug them, torture them, and sell them to others. There were plenty of people who wouldn't feel bad if my dad died. With ELEMENT, he did arrest quite a few traffickers, and he saved a lot of people, women and children and smuggled immigrants alike.

I didn't like thinking about his job much myself.

And for the most part, I could forget about everything entirely if I wanted, and as a teenager trying to survive school and juggle my extracurriculars, I did just that.

Until the incident.

One day, close to the end of the school year, I came home early. I was supposed to stay and play for the choir, since the spring concert was coming up, but Mrs. Nagy was out sick. As I walked into the apartment, I heard angry muffled voices coming from Mom and Dad's bedroom.

I frowned, before I realized Mom was yelling at Dad—something that had never, ever happened in all my memory of them together.

I was shocked, but I was even more stunned when I realized why she was upset.

"Jay, what is this? Are you in some kind of money trouble?" I heard Mom ask. She was practically weeping as I heard papers shuffling from their room. "What are all these tickets and vouchers? What on earth … why are you gambling like this?"

There was another pause before she added, "Why are you gambling like this with money like *that*?"

My knees started to shake; Dad was doing something egregiously wrong. I knew my parents had their faults, but it was the first time I really wondered if I'd end up as a statistic of some kind.

Mom began to pelt him with more probing questions as I regained my courage. I swallowed hard and then slid over to their bedroom door.

"Linda, please," Dad said. "Don't worry about this. I can't control everything in this world, but I want to make sure you and Stephen have money if you need it."

"We have some money saved!"

"Well, you might need more in the future," Dad insisted. "What about when Stephen wants to go to college? He's going to need it. Psychology degrees aren't cheap."

Mom gasped. "What?"

Dad cleared his throat. "… Assuming that's what he wants to go for, of course. There are plenty of things he can do at Georgia Tech, right?"

"Georgia Tech?" Mom sounded confused, and I was starting to get confused, too. "Did Stephen say something to you about Georgia Tech?"

No.

I wanted to say speak up, but I was still floundering. I hadn't said anything about college—I still had two full years of school to go, and I didn't know what I was going to do with my life.

"No, it's not that … not exactly," Dad said. "But what I mean is, what about after that? Wouldn't it be nice to be able to provide for our grandchildren one day?"

"We may not be rich, but we don't have any significant financial woes, Jay … and it's not like we're going to have grandchildren anytime soon. What's wrong, baby? Something's wrong. I can tell."

Mom's voice was cracking, almost like she was scared. "Tell me."

"Nothing's wrong, honey." Dad's tone was much less convincing.

I frowned and leaned against the door even more urgently. *What's going on? What are they talking about?*

"You could get in a lot of trouble for this," Mom said. "Betting like this isn't legal, is it?"

"As I said, don't worry about it. I have some contacts, and Ben's even agreed to help out. I made him promise," Dad said. "Look, all this is important to me, okay? You know me. I promise it's nothing about us, or Stephen. All I'm asking you to do now is trust me. That's all I can really say. For Stephen's sake, please don't question me on this."

I didn't hear the rest of their conversation, since Mom started crying and mumbling about how this had to be ELEMENT's fault. Dad started trying to comfort her, but his voice was still full of uncertainty.

Quickly, I turned and slipped away. My stomach was twisting with unease and guilt; I knew I'd heard something I wasn't supposed to, and I felt even more unsettled when reality sank in.

Dad was *gambling* with money … possibly illegally? With Ben's help, of all people?

Was it because of his new job—or something else?

Before I could wonder too much, Dad opened the door to their room, dressed for work.

"I've got to go," he called back over his shoulder. Mom was still grumbling in their room. "I'll be back late, so I'll see you then. I love you."

I heard Mom's stifled, "Love you, too," before Dad saw me.

Whatever anxiety he'd felt in arguing with my mom disappeared from his face. "Hey, son, didn't know you were home already." He spoke with a smile on his face, but there was a loneliness in his eyes as he looked at me. I noticed then that he seemed a little thinner than usual, and he even seemed older for some reason.

"Hey Pops," I murmured. I didn't know what to say; I wanted to ask him about his fight with Mom, but I didn't really want to know why.

"Guess what? I've told my boss all about you and she's got a surprise for us," he said. "She's certain you'll like it, too."

"Cool."

Dad patted me on the shoulder. "You'll have to come and meet her and everyone else down at HQ soon."

I thought about what Mom had said: ELEMENT was the reason he's acting so strange.

Was it possible there was a misunderstanding? Was it possible she'd gotten something wrong?

"Sure," I murmured again.

"Great!" Dad smiled. "I'll see you soon. I'm glad I caught you before work, but I gotta head out now. Have a good evening. I'll be home at the usual time tomorrow."

I glanced at the clock. Dad did work strange hours at times, but he didn't usually have twelve-hour shifts. "Aren't you early?" I asked.

"Oh. Well, I thought I'd go to church first," Dad explained. He sighed then. "There are a lot of unholy things I've seen of late, Stephen. When you see so much of evil, you should cling to God when you can. Otherwise evil starts to look attractive."

I nodded as he left, wondering if Mom was worried about that happening to Dad.

I wondered about that myself a moment longer, and then shook my head.

Dad wasn't like that, and he never would be.

Just like before, most of my worries went away, as school ended and I could indulge in summer vacation; Mom did private piano lessons while Dad kept working, so I had a lot more free time.

Gabe and I, along with some of our other friends, would play video games and hang out online. I still kept up my karate classes, and I was soon able to take other classes: self-defense, Japanese sword, Brazilian Jiu-Jitsu, and more.

Dad had promised me he'd take me to meet more people, and he kept it. One day, I went into the office to meet Dad's boss, Kathleen McKinley, who practically gushed over me. She seemed nice enough, and she got along well with Dad, or so it seemed to me.

While we were at Dad's office, I even got to meet Woodrow Hunter, the Director of ELEMENT. He was the one who oversaw the entire national division, and when he shook my hand, sized me up, and then nodded, I felt as though I'd passed some kind of test.

I felt important when I met them, and even if I wasn't interested in Dad's work, I enjoyed getting to see Dad was highly respected at his job, too.

But it was meeting Val Davis that ended up jarring me the most later on.

Dad introduced him to me as his new CPA, saying he'd sought him out to help him with his personal financial planning.

That struck me as odd, since he still had his pension with the police department, and even if Mom was worried about him gambling over Falcons games, she'd been right: We had enough money to live a good, upper-middle-class life, and we had enough saved away for emergencies. Besides all that, my parents had talked enough that even I knew ELEMENT had comprehensive insurance package with their benefits.

Why is Dad introducing me to his financial planner?

The longer I stood there, as Dad and Val chatted with each other, the more tension I felt in the air.

Something was wrong.

I gazed over at Dad, hoping for some clarity, but I was only further surprised to see him looking thoughtful and bitter as he watched Val.

As nonchalantly as possible, I studied Val myself; he was tall and lanky, much more slim than my dad, but still in good shape. He wore a nice suit and had his hair cut short. His glasses gave him a studious look, and while he slouched a little, there was a glimmer in his eye that hinted at his confidence, especially when it came to money.

"I'd like him to look after your accounts, too, one day, Stephen," Dad told me.

"I have accounts?" I asked, caught off guard by this. "But I'd just asked if I could get that new game system and you said—"

"Never mind that, son," Dad interrupted.

"It's good to meet you, Stephen," Val said as he shook my hand.

"Nice to meet you, sir," I said, giving him a small smile; Dad had always said that good manners would take you far, and offering respect invited others to give it to you. I might've been confused, but I was still going too polite.

"I'll need you to take good care of my boy, Val," Dad said, looking away. "And eventually my wife, too."

"Certainly, sir," Val agreed. "I've been doing this for several years, and I assure you, you can trust me."

"Thank you." Dad nodded before he glanced toward the small shelf of trophies on a high shelf. "I see you're quite competitive."

There were a number of first and second place trophies, all for shooting competitions. High caliber rifles, shotgun, and more.

"I was part of the school shooting team when I was young," Val explained almost sheepishly. "It's still one of my favorite hobbies."

Dad approved of this; he'd mentioned before he wanted me to learn how to shoot properly. "I have some friends who were talking about putting together

49

a firearms class down at the Atlanta Dojo," he told Val. "Perhaps you'd be interested in helping us out? I'm sure Stephen could learn a thing or two from someone like you, especially if I'm not there."

A chill went through my body.

"Why wouldn't you be there?" I asked.

Dad gave me an easy smile. "Well, I might have to work," he said smoothly enough. "And Ben will be only too eager to actually shoot someone. Sensei Shawn could use another hand in keeping things calmed down, don't you think?"

"I'd love to help," Val agreed, and he and Dad turned the conversation back to guns and ammo and their favorites as I stood there, not sure why I felt so uneasy and alone.

It was only much, much later I understood: I didn't know at the time that Val would one day be my stepfather—but Dad did.

*  *

I should've known better than to ignore all the strangeness happening around us. But just like before, it was too easy to slip back into the daily grind, especially as summer faded away, along with my free time, and then school started up again.

Eleventh grade was much easier than tenth already; Gabe was at my side, and while he did manage to reclaim some of his former fame, this time, he dragged me along with him. Everyone who'd once made fun of me for being a "piano boy" was impressed with my skills, and soon I had a small group of fangirls who followed me around constantly. The fact that my dad was no longer patrolling the city streets seemed to help, too; a lot more of my teachers and administration seemed to like me better, and I didn't know what to think of that. I'd grown up around cops—Dad, Ben, and his other friends on the force—and even at my age, it was disappointing to see so many adults struggle with nuance.

Still, I got used to it, and soon I didn't even want to remember my former life. Everything good just seemed to keep on coming.

Football season started up, and that's when everything especially came together in a beautiful way. One September day, I came home to see Dad was waiting for me with me a big smile on his face.

I briefly thought how rare they had become before he grabbed me up and hugged me.

"Guess what, Stephen," he cheered. "Kathleen's been talking around, and thanks to her, you've been selected as the student performer who's going to play the national anthem at the Falcons game this week!"

"What?" I straightened out my shirt as he put me down. "What are you talking about?"

"We're going to the game this week," he said. "And you're going as a special guest. You'll be playing the piano to kick off the game."

"Just playing?" I asked. "Someone going to be singing?"

"Oh, they've got someone else for that," Dad assured me. "Kathleen says they've made arrangements for the senator's daughter to sing."

"Senator?" I frowned, trying to remember who it was. "Which one?"

"Francesca Westlake-Hailey. She's the one who's married to the CDC director."

I tried to picture her face, but couldn't. Dad looked thoughtful. "Earlier this year she was accused of racketeering, remember?" he asked.

"No." Then I nearly laughed. "Oh, so you didn't vote for her, then?"

"It was between her or the one who was using his father-in-law's company to fund his campaign," Dad said neutrally, as though he expected me to remember who was who in politics. I didn't monitor that stuff; it would change every four to six years anyway.

At my frustrated look, he shrugged. "Either way, the game is supposed to have some big-time human traffickers there," Dad said. "There have been a lot of them popping up at games lately. With the big crowds and lots of strangers, it's easy for victims to get shuffled between handlers."

I swallowed hard. "I'll be okay, though?"

Dad smiled and put his hand on my shoulder. "I'm certain you'll be alright, son. You're going to be the star, playing right in front of everyone. No one's going to try to steal you."

"Sensei Shawn would be upset to know I couldn't handle myself," I agreed proudly. I was due to get another belt in karate soon, and I was already helping out with the beginner classes for jiujitsu.

"Exactly." Dad gave me a sad smile all of a sudden. "I'm glad you're doing so well, son."

"What's wrong?" I asked, suddenly worried again.

He shook his head. "I've got to go to work," he murmured, excusing himself. "Glad you're excited about the news. I'm sure your friends will be happy for you, too. Abby and Gabe and Sebastian, right?"

"Sebastian?" I frowned. "I don't know anyone named Sebastian."

"Oh. Right." Dad shrugged again, looking lost and gloomy, and also slightly afraid. "Well, maybe one day you will. Never mind me, son."

He turned away as Mom arrived home. She waltzed into the apartment, beyond cheerful to see we were both still home.

"Jay's already told me the news, Stephen," she said. "And I've already told the entire district that my baby's going to be a star! And a musician at that. I couldn't be prouder."

"Mom." I rolled my eyes.

"Come now, let me make a fuss," she insisted. "You're a good boy, Stephen. You've got good grades, you're making more friends, you haven't chosen a different girl to date each week, and especially none of those hussies who've been clinging to you from outside the music room—"

I blushed. "Mom."

"You know I'm right, just as you know you'll get more of them stalking you after they hear the news." She arched her brow at me, certain of her statement. "You've got a bright future ahead of you. Let me celebrate."

"Yes, let's celebrate." Dad reached forward and pulled Mom into an embrace. "You've made us both proud, son."

Mom continued to gush in agreement, but as I watched Dad, his eyes turned dark and he seemed depressed again. Mom's voice grew muffled as I wondered what was wrong.

What is his problem?

All the earlier troubles I'd sensed came rushing back; the gambling, the strange comments he'd make from time to time, meeting all the new people in our lives …

Some part of me didn't want to know why Dad was acting strange; some part of me was afraid to know.

It wasn't until the day of my performance that I understood—and even now, a decade later, I would give anything to go back and change it.

While the day of my performance seemed to approach in double-time, word of my upcoming stardom traveled through the school like wildfire. Mom was right about my fans. More appeared outside the music room, along with some new ones. Mom had been a music teacher for several years, so I guess she knew what was coming; still, I didn't tell her she'd been right—she already knew. She walked around the house with a smug look on her face, and if it had been because of anyone other than me, I would've been embarrassed.

I was embarrassed anyway, but I didn't mind as much, especially since Dad was acting stranger every day. One time, he came home while I was playing on my video game console, he just sat down and watched me play. He said nothing, but I gave him a smile, and he grinned back at me. We didn't talk much; Dad knew me well enough to know I didn't have a lot of performance issues, but I didn't enjoy the anticipation of them. My main method of dealing with my nerves was to push it all aside under several hours of gaming.

And then a few moments later, I glanced at him again. He was still smiling.

And then I'd only blinked, and suddenly his eyes were full of tears.

"What is it?" I asked.

"Nothing," he insisted, shaking it off. "I just need to get to the game early tomorrow. I need to talk to Kathleen about something, that's all."

"Nothing bad, is it?"

"Might be," Dad muttered, but he shrugged. Then he put on his bland, fake smile and ruffled my hair. "I'm going to go to church and pray a little."

"Again?" I sighed. "God must have some serious blackmail on you, Pops."

Dad chuckled. "Not blackmail, but blessings. You'll see what I mean one day. I know that for certain."

I rolled my eyes. Dad had always been insistent on church, and I never really cared that much. Since he began working for ELEMENT, he'd been going to church a lot more, and just then, I felt a twinge of warning in the back of my mind as I recognized he was genuinely worried about something.

Dad was already out the door before I could ask him anything.

I let him go and focused on my video game. I had a lot to worry about too, with my performance. I would be getting to meet the football players, I would get to meet the senator lady, and I would get to watch the game from the sidelines with Dad nearby.

It was a promise he'd been intent to fulfill.

"Dad doesn't need to worry so much," I murmured to myself.

I could not even begin to imagine how wrong I was.

* ♪ *

"Wow!" I hated how naïve and silly I sounded, looking around the Georgia Dome, but it was hard to contain myself. It was home of the Atlanta Falcons, the football stadium of the city, and I stood at the very top of it.

"Don't fall," Dad joked, as he came up beside me. He put his arm around my shoulder. "I didn't climb up this whole way here only for you to fall."

"Come on, you're not that old." I nudged him with my head, and he ruffled my hair affectionately.

"I'm old enough." He looked across the field, looking past the stadium onto the city. His eyes lost focus, as though he'd slipped into some unseen world. "I'm old enough to know you have a good future ahead of you, you know. You'll meet a nice girl one day, Stephen, and you'll have some great kids. And they'll love music, just as we do."

Finally, something broke inside of me. "What's up with you?" I asked. "Why you looking so scared, Dad? You're not the one playing here—my entire future will go down in flames if I mess up."

"It won't, for what it's worth. You'll do great." Dad gave me that forlorn smile of his again. "I already know."

"How?" I gave him a skeptical look. "You travel to the future or something?"

Dad looked stunned, as though I'd punched him. And then he sighed. "Not exactly."

"What do you mean?" I pressed, feeling more helpless and hapless than ever.

He shook his head. "We all have our troubles, son."

"I can't help you if you don't tell me what's wrong," I reminded him angrily.

"You're just nervous," Dad said, and I suddenly felt insulted and seen. "Pray with me?"

"Ugh." I groaned. "Come on, Dad … I'll be fine."

I wanted to tell him to snap out of his sad attitude, to tell me the truth, and to get a grip on reality.

But Dad didn't let me. He pulled me to his side again and held me there.

Silence settled between us, and I felt more afraid than ever.

"Pray for me, then," he said.

All I could do was nod.

He prayed for his life, for my own heart's steadfastness, for my mother's fortitude, and for the time we'd all shared together.

It was more eerie and ominous than comforting. As his prayer came to an end, I only felt more scared.

I opened my eyes, but kept my gaze down as I summoned my courage to ask Dad why things felt so wrong.

Before I could, there was a slight movement behind us.

"*Dad.*"

The voice was a whisper, deep and resonant, a low tenor that was familiar but foreign at the same time.

"Stay here, Stephen," Dad ordered, before he walked toward the shadows, toward the sound of the voice. "I need to check."

I glanced around and saw nothing—nothing at all. And then I blinked, and Dad was back, and he was coming toward me.

There was a resolved look on his face, something that was pleased but also terrified, but he was determined to face whatever was coming his way.

"Come on, son," he said, acting as though nothing unusual had happened at all. "Kathleen's down on the field, waiting for you. She's got everything set up, and she says Senator Westlake-Hailey is here, too."

My mouth felt dry, but I nodded. The nervousness I'd felt for my upcoming performance came rushing back, and I did my best to crush it down inside me again. I'd played before a crowd several times; surely this time wouldn't be too different.

Practicing for the national anthem was no big deal. While we did a sound check, I got to meet Senator Westlake-Hailey, and Dad's boss, Kathleen, was there, too. Kathleen's reddish-brown curls were practically bouncing as she talked. She was excited that she'd been able to put all this together for me and Dad and the senator.

Senator Francesca Westlake-Hailey was more concerned with the performance. I finally recognized her somewhat, recalling her commercials for when she was running for senator. She was tall, with larger black cornrow braids down her back, but still wearing the political pantsuit style popularized in the 90s by hard-hitting women politicians. It didn't matter if I was pleased or not to see her; she just assumed I was one of her fans and then hurriedly busied herself with other things. She shook my hand, very briefly, as her dark brown eyes glazed over, and she started yelling about the lighting and the sound and all that right in her next breath. I didn't want to bother with her much myself, but she didn't even hear me say, "Bye," when she turned away from me.

"She doesn't like cops much," Kathleen whispered. She came up beside me and put her hand on my shoulder. She nodded toward Dad, who was watching everything from off to the side. "Thank you for being polite."

"No problem," I assured her with a shrug. "I get it."

"She also wants everything to be perfect for her daughter," Kathleen added, still watching the senator as she bossed more people around. Suddenly, Kathleen let out a small, sarcastic laugh. "I'm sure Harmony is thrilled."

At her words, I glanced over at the senator's daughter.

Harmony Westlake was supposed to be about twelve years old, and she looked every part the perfect child star. She wore an impeccable, simple dress with a red sash that matched her shoes—and her mother's shoes, too, I noticed. Her hair was black like her mother's, but much smoother, and it was pulled back into pigtails. She watched her mother without any inflection on her face, and for a long moment, I wondered if she was nervous at all.

Harmony's eyes flickered over to me. Instantly, I turned away, embarrassed I'd been caught staring.

I glanced back at her a moment later, only to find she was still staring at me. Her gaze was no longer empty, but one of curiosity, and it was nice to see she had some personality.

Her mother came up to her a second later, reprimanding her for losing her focus, and I turned back Dad.

"Well, seems everything's in order," I murmured, and he nodded.

"Kathleen's made sure everything will work out alright," he said, pulling me after him. "Now, let's go find our seats and watch the game!"

Dad was still serious and somehow forlorn, but His promise to me was finally getting fulfilled, and he was full of excitement.

His mood was contagious, and I soon found myself swept up alongside him. The crowds were coming in, the players were warming up, the cheerleaders were heading out; music began to swell within the stadium.

I don't remember much of anything from those last moments before Harmony and I were called to perform. I was swamped with emotions—anxiety, fear, and uncertainty, but also hope, pride, and excitement.

Somehow, I made it down to the field entrance, with Dad guiding me as people cheered and the crowds were on their feet. I walked up the long, dark hallway, standing to the one side.

Dad clapped me on the shoulder. "You'll do great, son. Don't be scared. It's time to be brave."

I nodded. "Thanks, Dad."

He slipped back down the hallway—he was still working a job, after all—and I took a deep breath, trying to steady myself.

This is the performance of a lifetime …

"Alright, Harmony," a voice said to the side of me. "Now, remember what we've practiced. Don't forget to project, make sure you're standing tall and proud, and don't mess up. You don't want to make me look bad, right?"

I glanced over, awkwardly watching as Harmony looked down at her shoes, a pained expression on her young face.

"I won't disappoint you."

Harmony murmured the words, and I suddenly felt so bad for her.

"Well, you better not," Senator Westlake-Hailey agreed with a large, fake-smile on her face. "I'm already down several polling points, and I need a win if I'm going to keep my job in the senate. If I don't, you know what that means … we'll be out on the streets and into the poorhouse before you know it, and that means you'll lose your singing lessons and all your pretty clothes, and shoes, and books, and … "

The list rattled on, and I felt more embarrassed than ever to be listening into a conversation. I was almost glad that the announcer called everyone to attention for the National Anthem.

"And now singing the National Anthem is Harmony Westlake, the daughter of Georgia Senator Francesca Westlake-Hailey … "

At the senator's name, there was a large mix of "boos" and tepid clapping from the stands.

I guess she wasn't lying about her poll numbers. I glanced over to see Harmony was standing alone.

She was standing tall and straight and proud, just as her mother wanted. But I could see her sadness and weariness in her eyes, and if we'd have had a moment, I might've said something to cheer her up some.

But then they called my name, too, and Harmony and I walked out together.

The cheering picked up a little, but I'm not sure if it was for me or just because people could see Harmony was just a child, really, and she didn't deserve her mother's ire.

I took my place at the piano and took another deep breath. Beside me, Harmony gave me a look, and I smiled at her, and nodded to let her know I was ready.

She seemed taken aback a little, as if she was surprised; I didn't know why, but she smiled a little more brightly, and I was close enough to her that I could see it was genuine.

For some reason, that made me relax more than anything else.

I put my hands down on the keys, and began to play, and Harmony began to sing.

It was a surreal moment, where I felt every fiber of my being cry out in amazement; I was on the stage, playing before thousands of people, being broadcast all throughout the nation, taking my place in music history.

I felt peace, I felt confidence; I felt the pure beauty of that moment surround and reverberate into the deepest reaches of my soul … in that moment, the universe seemed to open up and give me the smallest glimpse of all the power, light, and love it had to offer. For the first time in my life, I had an inkling as to why Dad loved music so much, and his love of music became my own.

As I played the last keys, and Harmony's last note fell into silence, I breathed out a prayer of thanks.

"Thank you, God," I whispered, still full of wonder.

I glanced back toward the hallway; I saw my dad looking proud and content.

I stood up and bowed, while Harmony curtsied, and then we made our way back off the field. She stopped to get some roses and bouquets that some of the nearby people tossed her way—I briefly wondered if they were paid to do so, thanks to her mother.

Once I was out of the audience's view, I started running.

"Dad!" I called, so happy and full of excitement. I saw him approach me, and I opened my arms when Kathleen suddenly stepped in front of me and walked right into me.

She embraced me hard, surprising me. "Oh, Stephen!" she practically cooed. "You did such a wonderful job! Your dad was right; you have a super talent."

"Oh, uh, thank you so much, ma'am," I said, awkwardly hugging her back. I glanced over to see Dad walk out toward the entrance, waiting for Harmony to come under the bleachers, too.

Kathleen hugged me again, making me feel unsettled. "We will have to find a way to have you play again for us, Stephen. Wouldn't that be great?"

"Really?" I thought of that moment, and my eyes lit up with all the dreams of fame, fortune, and adoring fans a sixteen-year-old could conjure. "That would be amazing. Is that really possible?"

I was just about to ask Dad what he thought when I saw the gun come out of the shadows behind us.

In the next second, I went from confused to unsure to scared, and I couldn't say anything.

"Stop," Dad called out, reaching for his own gun.

But before he could shoot, the man who held the gun reached for Harmony. He took her and dragged her off the field, and in the background, I could hear the crowd murmuring in bewilderment. Some part of me wondered if this was a trick; maybe I'd fainted and I didn't play at all, or maybe I was stuck at some hospital on life support, or dealing with a severe concussion …

But then, Harmony screamed, and I snapped out of it. "Help!"

"Shut up," the man's gravel-like voice shouted at her.

Kathleen grabbed onto me, trying to keep me away. "Stay still," she ordered. "It's for your own good. It's The Marxman!"

"No," I argued, pushing her away more harshly than I'd meant. I broke free and began to run. I had no choice; Harmony was in trouble, and Dad was, too.

Dad was already moving into action, and it was at that moment I knew things were going to go horribly, unspeakably wrong.

The man with the gun—"The Marxman," as Kathleen had called him—now held the gun up and aimed as my Dad pulled Harmony free.

I saw the man's finger squeeze.

"No!" I shouted, as if to demand God stop time himself to save my father.

But it was not meant to be.

Dad crumbled to the ground, his chest suddenly full of blood. I reached for him as The Marxman snatched Harmony again.

Kathleen put her hand to her mouth. "I'm calling for an EMT, Jay," she called, hurrying away. "Hold on!"

I started to run toward The Marxman, who let go of Harmony to handle me.

I couldn't make out his face in the shadows, but I did all I could to keep him from leaving my grasp.

"What's the holdup? One girl isn't too much for you, is she?" A new voice grumbled out from the other side of the hallway. The voice was similar to The Marxman, in a demonic way, and without explanation, I knew they were partners. They were here to kidnap Harmony.

"Shut up, Nolan," The Marxman shot back. "Some stupid kid here's tryin' to play hero." He kicked me, and if my eyes hadn't been so full of tears, I might've dodged it.

"Come on, I've got the senator's girl," the other man said, as The Marxman tossed me into the wall. My vision swam, but not before I saw the other shadow grab hold of Harmony.

"Stop it," Harmony yelled, squirming as she was once more getting dragged away. "Stop it, please! I haven't done anything to you. I'm innocent!"

The man holding her, who I assumed was Nolan, laughed. "That's why you'll fetch a high price in our markets, little lady."

The two men started to run; more sirens and whistles rang out, but no one was nearby that could do anything.

No one but me.

But …

"Dad." I gasped out his name as he lay on the ground, holding his chest, whimpering silently, trying to be brave in the face of pain.

"Stephen," he rasped. "Go save the girl."

"No! I won't leave you."

Dad gave me a small smile. "I'll be alright. Now, go get your girl, son. She needs you more than I do."

"Someone else can get her!"

"No, son," Dad said, more sternly than I'd expected. "If we don't step up and help, no one will. Now, go!"

I frowned at him, but his voice oddly calmed me. I was able to stand up and I started running; I could still see both The Marxman and his accomplice, heading down the hallway and making a break for the exit. One of them went to the right where the storage exit was, and the other one, the one with Harmony in his arms, went to the left, where the crowded concession stand lines would slow him down.

Faced with the option, I made up my mind almost instantly; the Marxman had shot my dad, and I would get him first. Surely there would be plenty of people who would stop the other man.

But before I could go too far, a foot reached out and tripped me.

I fell forward at full-speed, careening down the hard cement of the hallway. "What in the world?" I yelped.

The new shadowed figure was already a gold and black blur against the walls. All I knew for certain was that it was another man, and I'd never seen him before.

"Save the girl! I'll get the killer," the man called. His voice was a little familiar, but it wasn't anything like The Marxman's or his partner's voice.

I didn't know what else to do … so I did what I was told. I headed out after Harmony and her kidnapper, wondering if I could get a glimpse of The Marxman again.

I raced outside to see Harmony getting hauled up a long flight of stairs; it was the way toward one of the north gates, and I'd seen it earlier, when Dad and I had come in with Kathleen. There were some other people around, but no one seemed to notice what was happening.

Not knowing what else to do, I called out. "Hey! Stop!"

Behind me, I could hear Kathleen's voice. "There's the kidnapper!"

Police whistle sounded out, and the man turned around. He wore his long black hair back in cornrows, and his matching goatee was cut sharply across his face. At my voice, he whirled around; he had a frown on his face, and it deepened as he saw all of us chasing him.

Suddenly, he stumbled; his foot turned, and he went off-balance. In that second, he dropped Harmony.

She tumbled away from him, struggling to keep herself from falling down. She flailed her arms as she fell back, screaming.

I jumped forward, desperate to save her, as Dad had wanted.

I caught her just in time. She grabbed onto me, her hands shaking as she looked up at me, her eyes wide and scared.

Behind us, the police managed to catch up to the kidnapper.

"Well, well, well," one of the policemen said. "It's Nolan Cameron, the famous child trafficker!"

"What's he doing in such a public place?" Another policeman asked. "Seems unusual."

"Football games are great places for kids to get lost," the first policeman replied as he got out his handcuffs.

That's when I stopped listening. Harmony was starting to whimper.

Harmony grabbed onto me even more tightly. "You saved me," she gasped, surprised and happy and still terrified beyond belief. Tears flooded her eyes and she cried into my chest.

I didn't even notice; I was too busy watching the EMTs and Kathleen and the police.

Dad's body was unnaturally still as the EMTs worked.

I knew he was gone.

He was gone, and my life would never be the same after that.

* ♪ *

After Dad died, the following days once more blurred over. My life was swamped in sadness, and I was unable to handle just how painful the present was in those moments.

I felt compelled to take care of my mom, and she seemed to welcome my help, for the most part. Over the next few days, I would make her eat dinner and I would sit near her whenever she just wanted to mourn. There were a lot of things that had to happen after Dad's death—certainly a lot more than I was expecting. It was hard to find rest and even more difficult to feel certain I was doing what I should've been doing. It helped that Mom let me stay home from school, and she took a leave of absence herself while she organized Dad's funeral and worked with Val to sort out Dad's will and life insurance policy.

For days, I suffered, replaying that moment when the shadowed hand had reached out and shot my dad while his partner kidnapped Harmony. I would dream about it, vividly, and I would wonder if I could've changed anything.

I wallowed in self-hatred, self-doubt, and self-disgust.

But then, seven days later, I had a moment of true clarity, and my life changed once again.

I was at Dad's funeral, where, as the priest was praying for my father's eternal rest, I was suddenly once more surrounded by music. It was just like I'd felt at the game.

The music swelled in my soul; it wasn't the National Anthem, but it was something greater—it was the Anthem of Heaven itself, and it was then I started to see the different songs inside each soul.

I didn't know what exactly had happened just then, but it was the first inkling of an unfolding symphony.

I couldn't explain it to anyone; even when I asked Mom about it, she suggested therapy, and I complied so she wouldn't worry. It was in therapy I started to think about my future, about how I could use my pain to serve my purpose, and to help others.

It was then I started to form a plan.

I was given a gift for a reason, and I would use it responsibly and righteously.

I formed an ambitious plan, one that would require focus and discipline and training—but it was worth it.

Over the years, I learned to harness my power, control it, and even help it grow. I started to see not only the music of each soul, but their feelings, and then their memories. If I wanted to, I could even work on changing their emotions.

I had a gift to comfort and confront, to encourage and to intervene. I could do a lot of good, but I could also cause a lot of trouble.

Knowing that, I still made my choice.

As the years passed, I remember thinking it was almost as if Dad had known; that was why he'd been gambling over games, that was why he'd opted for the best life insurance coverage possible, that's why he made sure ELEMENT would pay Mom and me well in the event of his death.

And then there were other little things that made me wonder if he'd known.

There were brochures in his nightstand for counselors, including a man named Dr. Hammersley, who specialized in therapy for child trauma and family loss. He was the one Mom sent me to for therapy and counseling.

Dad had given Sensei Shawn ten years' worth of tuition for me to continue learning at his dojo. Val stepped in and talked with Mom for long hours over our family's finances, and he'd mentioned once about how Dad had set up a tuition fund for me. He even set up some extra accounts for me, but Val said they were sealed under protection until I reached a certain age.

Dad also hooked Father Mike into his plans, too. The kindly priest would make sure I'd show up to church and I kept up with my piano lessons, even when Mom lost nearly all her affection for it.

I couldn't blame her; it reminded her too much of Dad.

She felt she'd lost him, but for me, music was the ultimate sign that I hadn't; Dad was still there, with his people surrounding me, offering me little notes to guide me along the way.

My gift was just that—a gift, and it was one I would use to soothe the pain in others' hearts as well as my own.

I started to learn how to control my musical powers. I worked hard to train my body. I went to church to ask for guidance. I took care of my mom. I finished school.

I dreamed of better days ahead.

I vowed to stand for justice and protect the innocent. I promised I would never lose sight of what was really important.

And after almost ten years, when I finally took to the streets as Dizchord, I was more than ready.

Because that's what Dad would've wanted me to do—and that's what I wanted, too.

74

CHAPTER THREE

* ♪ *

back to the present …

"Thanks for the help. Sorry we were a little late."

I half-smile at the resigned tone of Ben's voice. In the past ten years, it's only gotten more surly and more deep—likely thanks to all the cigarettes he liked to smoke, courtesy of chronic stress—but time had not dulled Ben's pride in the least. If anything, he was a walking, one-man institution of Atlanta's police department, and he earned his distinction.

Remembering this, I lean back a little and cross my arms, hiding my face from him as much as I can. It's almost strange to see him in his same old uniform; I can't help but wonder if he's gotten passed over for another promotion recently.

"You were almost too late," I say, daring to poke the beast a little.

"Well, that's Atlanta traffic for you." He nonchalantly lights a cigarette as he turns off his body camera. His eyes flicker to mine, and I nod in acknowledgement.

Ben doesn't know it's me under my mask, and he would be appalled if he did; but he and I have run into each other before on a few of my missions, and right away, he'd seemed to sense we were on the same side.

Mostly, anyway—at least enough that we could work together.

And Ben, despite being the same old straight-as-an-arrow, stick-in-the-mud cop I'd always known, chose to work with me, even though it's against the books.

I knew he would—for the sake of the victims, if nothing else.

"Any of these kids look familiar?" I ask, already knowing the answer.

Ben shakes his head curtly. "No. I'd guess they're all illegals, most likely. Border Patrol weak and that's when all these kids get assigned 'guardians' disguised as real, regular people."

"Most trafficking clients are disguised like that," I agree, watching as an EMT looks over the boy I'd comforted earlier. I hear him asking about his mom, and I think of my own mother in that moment.

Mom doesn't know where I am, and if she did, she would have a heart attack by now.

There's a loud grumbling noise behind us, and I watch as one of the thugs I'd beaten up earlier is put into handcuffs and led away.

I narrow my eyes; Bernard Marcello must've managed to get away.

He's escaped.

I bite down on the inside of my cheek in a flash of frustration; after a moment, I let my anger go. I lightly mention Marcello's involvement to Ben; he makes his own grumbling noises and agrees to make note of it, but without physical evidence he can turn in, we both know there's nothing he can really do.

If nothing else, I'll find Marcello again at some point.

God willing, I would anyway; Marcello needs to get off the streets, just like the rest of the traffickers.

"I'm glad you found them," Ben continues, taking another long inhale from his cigarette. "We've got new protocols on the force."

"New protocols?" I frown, recalling how Dad had always hated those, too.

"Technically, we're not supposed to investigate without reasonable cause, but that's been redefined thanks to Her Ladyship."

I raise my eyebrow, taken aback at Ben's clear disdain. He's obviously annoyed, but I'd always known him as a seasoned professional.

Perhaps it's because he's older, or because he doesn't know who I am, but it's strange to hear him mock the governor.

"You know how it is with politics." Ben rolls his eyes, seeing my confusion. "Her Ladyship, Governor Westlake-Hailey, is particularly unhappy with police performance. We have more paperwork to process before answering a call. She's a downright tyrant about it, too."

"I'll try to tip you off earlier in the future," I promise, even though I know it will be tricky to do just that.

A new thought strikes me as we stand there. If there are protocols in place that slow down the response process, there are likely more ways to kill the call altogether, too.

I wonder if the policemen were encouraged to turn a blind eye with things like this. I consider asking Ben outright, but I remain silent for now; Governor Westlake-Hailey might've had her problems to deal with—but I have my own, too.

And I've been waiting ten years to get this close to solving them.

"Just take care of the kids for me," I say, taking a step forward.

It's time for me to seek out The Marxman, the man who'd killed my father.

As much as it pains me to leave the kids behind, I need to find the answers to my questions—and that means I have to find him.

"Will do." Ben gives me the barest glimpse of a vulnerable, grateful look. "I can't admit it publicly, but I appreciate your help. I can file this under 'vigilante crime,' to keep her Ladyship happy in the governor's office."

"I know," I tell him quietly.

He nods, and we have another unspoken understanding.

"Any other requests?" he asks.

Each time we've met, he's asked me this, and tonight is the first time I take advantage of it.

"Yes," I say, clearly surprising him. "Let me take care of her for a few moments."

I nod toward Kathleen, who is huddled on the ground, wrapped up in a blanket. She's still terrified by the power I'd used in calling up her worst nightmares and memories, and I can't feel bad for her while looking at the kids nearby.

Ben hesitates before he lets out a reluctant sigh. "You're not going to do anything … bad, are you?"

I scoff, unable to stop myself from feeling insulted. "Worse than she's already done tonight? No."

"What do you need her for?" Ben gives me a cautious, curious look, and I almost smile.

I know what he really wants to ask.

The moniker "Dizchord" wasn't my first choice for a name—the Atlanta news media conglomerate had given it to me after some of the traffickers I helped send to prison reported how I'd taken them down. Honestly, I didn't really mind it, and I've never tried to correct them or change it, even after I saw the awkward spelling. There will always be assumptions about people, whether they're based on race, biology, religion, or other things. I was just glad that the name seemed to match my abilities.

I'd never bothered to help anyone understand my power; I'd only vaguely described it to Mom and Dr. Hammersley, as well as Father Mike on occasion. I'd get a grim look from Mom, who likely thought I was going insane after Dad's passing, curious interest from Dr. Hammersley, and half-awe and half-suspicion from Father Mike. None of them had ever spoken to others of my power, as far as I can tell, but I'm not really sure they believe it's real, either.

Thankfully, even the media thinks actual superpowers is too much a stretch for their credibility.

But as Ben looks at me though, I feel my resolve weaken, just a little; I'm tempted to confirm his suspicions, if for no other reason than because I know he misses my dad, too.

But instead, I frown. "I need to find her boss yet. The Marxman." I glance around, suddenly wondering if he's watching us even now.

"The Marxman?" Ben gasps, clearly taken aback. "He's the one who murdered my best friend. I didn't know he was coming here tonight."

"He's due to check in," I murmur. Gabe had mentioned that with the bigger order of kids coming in, only the Marxman's most trusted goons would be in charge of their drop-off.

Ben's face is pale and his knuckles are white against the darkness. "I've been tracking him for years," he says with a sigh.

I nod toward Kathleen. "This lady here is one of his higher-ups. He's likely to check in with her. I want to see if she can lead me to him."

Ben looked thoughtful. "He's been in the business for a long time," he says carefully. "I'm sure he's survived for a reason. Be careful, won't you?"

"Then we have an agreement?" I ask.

"Yes." He's still in shock, but he puts out his cigarette and turns on his body camera again. "I'll see to the kids."

I nod, and half a second later, I swoop down, grab a shivering, whimpering Kathleen off the ground, and then I hustle out of there.

"No," she moans as I toss her over my shoulder. I'm a little surprised; she's frailer than I thought, and lighter, too.

I try to push back all the sympathy I feel for her; as despicable as she is, it's still harder than I'd like.

I slide through the streets, heading just a little ways up from the old train station. I don't go far; I know I'll need to dump her back off with Ben before the night is over. I also don't go too far since the whole time I'm carrying her, she's moaning and groaning and begging to be put down.

"Can't you stop?" she whines. "All that noise in my head … the clashing and the clanging. What did you do to me? I feel sick."

"It's not anything I did," I say, slowing down a bit. She goes silent for a moment, likely surprised I'd said something to her at all.

Part of me suddenly wonders if she recognizes me. I doubt it, but for the first time, I falter.

I'd never used my powers on a woman like that; Kathleen, while she was the complete opposite of my mother, was still a woman, and Dad had raised me to take care of them. Perhaps that's why I feel compelled to explain myself, if only a little.

"Each person is born with a song inside their soul," I explain slowly. "It ebbs and flows with your life. It changes with your thoughts, your feelings, your will … every choice you make affects the melody inside of you."

"That doesn't explain what you did to me," Kathleen grumbles.

"My gift is that I can hear that song, and I can make you hear it, too," I say.

"I don't believe you." She snorts loudly, and then moans again. "Put me down."

"Okay."

She seems shocked when I finally do place her down against another wall. She's further surprised when I kneel before her, reaching out with one hand.

She jerks back away from me, but it's to no avail. My power lights up into my palm. My gloves are thin and strong, but it still lets the light shine. She sees it, too; her eyes are wide with disbelief as I touch her forehead.

At once, my power surges into her, and I can hear her soul song once more. It's loud and obnoxious and toxic, but it's also full of hurt and loss and failed hopes and dreams.

Digging through her inner discord is a chore; I mentally sift through her memories, calling up the images of the ones that are hiding, the ones that are loud, and the ones full of grief and sorrow.

"You say you don't believe me," I tell her. "But how do I know your father left you and your mother when you were only eight?"

Her eyes fill with tears, and I feel my own sympathy grow as I see more pain, sadness, and loss.

"How do I know your stepfather abused you?" I ask, hating how sorry I feel for her already. "How do I know you left home when you were only fifteen?"

I see more memories; the abuse in her childhood is like a large tsunami, crashing down on her self-image, her self-care, and her self-respect. I can watch as she latches onto prestige and power, seeking out wealth, getting involved with drug trades, trafficking, and affairs. I watch as she sells herself, one decision at a time, before she's caught and "reformed" and then hired by ELEMENT.

The man who talks with her looks familiar, but I can't quite place him. He's got wheat-colored hair that's balding on his head, large, gentle eyes that narrow sharply into slits, and a stocky build that commands respect in a domineering way.

Perhaps … he's a coworker? A pimp? Another trafficker?

Kathleen struggles against me, breaking into my concentration.

"You could've learned all that from a report," she objects.

I say nothing as I find a familiar memory—the day my dad died. I watch as a shadowed man yells at her, telling her she shouldn't have gotten involved with Harmony's kidnapping—and that *I* could've been captured, too.

Kathleen says it would have caused too much trouble, both with the press, and with her new boyfriend. She tells the man she especially didn't want to cause him any issues, since they'd just started their relationship.

The man huffs at her angrily, telling her Jay only had one kid, his wife wouldn't know how to get him back, and there were plenty of clients who would've liked a piano boy to play with, especially the son of a government agent and former cop.

Kathleen turns around as he yells something muffled at her, but she storms out of the room, unrepentant.

The memories fade, and the earlier rage I'd felt at Kathleen subsides, if only minimally, as I realize something truly astounding.

Harmony wasn't the only one who'd been at risk—I was supposed to have died or been kidnapped, too.

Kathleen *had* protected me that day, and she'd done so against her own business interests.

I slide back away from Kathleen, just slightly, as I maintain my composure.

Thanks to my power, I've learned several times over, both gratefully and begrudgingly, that its best not to act out in anger, even if it feels justified. Good judgement requires a broad perspective, and no single human is qualified to give it.

I hate how I'm reminded of this all over again, faced with the lady who orchestrated Dad's death.

"Here's something that's not in a report," I murmur quietly. "The day Jaayli Kibwaa was murdered by The Marxman, you still tried to protect his son."

"Oh my God." Kathleen's eyes went wide and dark.

She stared at me, and I stare back. Part of me hates to see that she knows she's done wrong things in her life, and she still wants to make it right.

I feel sorry for her, and sick for myself.

There's nothing she can do to make up for my dad's loss.

And that's just *one* thing she's done, too. There are countless other choices she's made that have only led her further into darkness.

"Finally believe me now?" I ask.

Kathleen doesn't have a coherent response. She's whimpering again, and I shake my head.

It's time to get down to the main business I came here for.

"Now that you understand me better … and I know you better, too … Tell me, where's your boss?"

Kathleen finally gets her gumption back as she sneers.

Her eyes are angry and vindicated, and she's ready to pay me back for her trouble.

"So … this was a trap," I whisper quietly, making her tremble again.

She slumps over as I hear a distinctive *click* behind me.

I straighten my shoulders and stand up, letting Kathleen scramble back from me.

"There's no need to hide," I say, calling on my power. Already, I can feel The Marxman's soul behind me, as grimy and dirty as it is. I nearly flinch at the ugliness, and I prepare to stomach more.

"What's the point, if you know me already?" The Marxman asks, and I have to give him credit. I'd underestimated his intelligence; using Gabe and my own research, I didn't think he'd know I was chasing after him.

"You're right," I tell him. "I do know you … Martin Cameron."

He pauses.

"Or should I saw Martin Hubbard?" I say. "I finally found you after I learned you're Nolan Cameron's half-brother."

"You're the guy who's been interrupting Kathy's cargo dumps, aren't you?" he growls.

He scoffs, but I can see his hand tightening around his gun as I turn to face him.

This is the man I'd been looking for, subconsciously or intentionally, for the last ten years.

This is the man who'd shot my father without a second thought.

This is the man I had to bring down.

For some reason, I'm not afraid of him. He's older than I'd imagined, he's even frailer than I'd thought. Fear has a strange effect on the imagination, and for some reason I thought I'd feel more closure as I came face to face with my father's killer.

But I don't.

I only feel rage and a strange bout of relief.

The dual reaction grows as I see Martin—The Marxman himself—flinch; he seems unusually unnerved to see me. Even in the shadows, I watch as his face blanches over.

For some reason, he seems to recognize me, although I'm not sure why.

At this, I frown in confusion.

Perhaps he's got his own sources? Why is he so agitated?

Martin swallows hard. "All those coyotes and pimps sure would like to get ahold of you, you know."

The song of his soul waves with wariness as he watches me.

"I thought you were just some do-gooder at first," he murmurs, clearly frightened now.

But why? Again, I wonder if it's Kathleen's whimpering form that makes him step back, or if it's something else.

Martin shifts his weight, trying to put forth a show of confidence. "But you're not … you were looking for me, all this time, weren't you? I'll admit, I didn't think you'd find me after all these years. I've been at this for the last decade, and I thought it was impossible."

"No." I shake my head. "It was inevitable."

Martin nearly chokes; but a moment later, he clears his throat and finally holds up his gun. "Yes, but only because I've let you."

He's lying, but I don't expect a villain to tell the truth.

"The resemblance between you and Nolan is uncanny," I tell him, eager to keep him on his toes.

"Ha!" Martin laughs. "I'm much more handsome than he is. Kathy would be the first to tell you so, too—assuming you didn't shatter her mind completely."

"She'll make a full recovery." I gaze down at her briefly. "Assuming she actually wants to."

In that moment, I suddenly wonder if I'd be able to see into her future. Using my power, I'm able to see into the past, the memories tied to the human heart and the music of the soul. But it would be interesting to see if she really could change her ways, to see if she could make better choices for herself.

Having grown up in church, I knew it was possible for such miracles to happen.

Almost as if she hears my thoughts, Kathleen struggles to stand up.

I ignore her, turning back to The Marxman. "You know, being the second-ugliest man alive isn't much of a bragging point. You can only at least say you're not in jail like he is—yet."

The Marxman snarls at my comments, and I call forth my power. His soul is twisted and deeply scarred, damaged and mauled beyond feeling. I feel the stinging proudness of his anger, and I prepare myself to make a move.

But before either of us do anything, Kathleen steps forward and shields me.

"Wait, Martin," she begs. "We can't kill him."

Both Martin and I are caught off guard by her comments.

"His power is real," she whispers, almost too afraid to admit it. "Maybe we could bring him to our side. Just imagine what Selena will think. We can find a way to do new things."

I can see her soul song spark with hope; I can see she remembers the day she saved me from The Marxman before.

I'm shocked; she doesn't even know who I am, but I can see she still wants to find a way back to being a good person—she wants a way to pay for her mistakes, and find out if she can be redeemed.

And all because I'd reminded her of how she'd chosen to save me.

Martin grumbled. "This isn't the first time you've gotten in my way, Kathy," he says.

"I know we disagree at times about what is best, honey," Kathleen argues, her voice breaking.

As she speaks, I realize Martin is the one who'd been her lover, even ten years ago when my dad died. She's argued with him and for him, and it's cost her promotions and kept her under his watch as part of their business.

Kathleen tries to speak again. "Perhaps if we just call Selena—"

"No." Martin interrupts her again, much more harshly than expected. It's clear they've had this confrontation before, and he's had enough. "I'm sorry, but you're delusional, Kathy."

I'm already moving as his fingers squeeze the trigger.

Kathleen is too slow, and she goes down hard. Her eyes are full of tears as they stare blankly into the nothingness of death. Her soul song disappears, its light and music flickering out in the wink of an eye.

I don't know why I'm sad to see her dead.

My fingers curl into fists. "You didn't have to do that!"

I shout at The Marxman louder than I'd meant to, but it doesn't matter. He seems more than a little shocked himself.

Maybe he'd finally gone too far himself, and he sees it's too late for him to turn back now …

His old, harsh face hardens as he glares up at me, but his gun is still shaking. "You mean *she* didn't have to do that!" he insists, already rewriting the events of the night as he steps back from me.

I see the notes of his soul's inner song radiate out from him, full of fear and shame and sadness.

"Our loyalty to Selena is required to be above reproach! A man will swim the world's oceans for a woman he loves, but he'll damn her a thousand times over to keep from being damned himself."

Martin shoots his gun at me, as if to add some weight to his words.

But his aim's off and his thoughts all in disarray; I easily avoid the bullets, although the gunshots echo loudly and clearly into the night.

Ben will not be happy about this.

I grimace, realizing that Kathleen's death will be seen as my fault, and if I don't get The Marxman into custody, I'll have more trouble than ever to worry about.

Martin takes off as the gunshots pause, and as he runs away, he lets out a disturbing laugh.

He could be crazy, he could be insane, he could be full of tragic despair. The notes surrounding him grow dark and silent, and then, much like Kathleen's, they flicker out, too.

In that moment, I think of my dad.

Kathleen wasn't the only one who'd died because of The Marxman.

Rage crests through my body like a resounding crescendo.

He might feel bad, but he should *feel bad! He killed my dad!*

Immediately, I run.

I run after him, hard and fast.

My hands grip the rungs of the old ladder he's climbing.

Much like that day in the Georgia Dome, I feel a sense of the divine; my fingers are fast and nimble as I climb. My footsteps are light and my body is limber as I move.

We reach the top of a building, and I feel certain I've got the upper hand.

He turns around and prepares to shoot again, but it's easy enough for me to deliver a right hook to his face.

The Marxman tries to fight back, but he's still reeling from my first punch.

My sense of confidence grows. Sensei Shawn's teaching has served me well for the last ten years, and I make my advance.

There's another uppercut to the front, and a left hook this time.

Without his gun, he's nothing!

Another kick sends him flying back, and he teeters on the edge of the roof.

His eyes are wide and scared as he fumbles backward, and for a long, slow split-second, I think about just letting him fall.

But the split-second passes, and I lunge for him.

I grab him by the collar and hoist him up high, letting him choke on his good fortune as the rage inside me calls for blood.

It's too easy to imagine squeezing the life out of The Marxman myself.

It's too easy to picture my dad's body, unnaturally still on the ground, covered in blood.

I don't realize how tightly I'm holding him until he's coughing, struggling to breathe against my hold.

He finally grabs my hands and gazes up at me, almost gleeful to see me so close.

"What're you waiting for?" he taunts. "Kill me already!"

It's so tempting.

I can taste the sinful flurry of his death; I can feel the delight inside me calling for its sustenance.

Slowly, I put his feet back on the ground.

"No," I grumble angrily. "I wish I could, but I can't."

"Too scared to shed a little blood yourself, are you?" The Marxman laughs at me.

He starts coughing again as my hand tightens around his neck.

"No." I loosen my grip only minimally as I call on my power. "Too sensible. I need you for information."

At once, I can see into his mind. The music is hollow and haunted, but I can see into his past and his heart.

It's not a surprise to see that he's always felt poor and powerless.

That's where the woman he's called Selena came in, easily enough; she's offered him money to take care of her "special deliveries" of children and women and more.

He's always felt lonely, too hardened by life.

That's where Kathleen reached out to him; the two of them were both lonely souls, looking out for their survival, but even more so, searching for a way out of their evil.

He's always been bullied and hated by others; he's always been outcast and afraid.

Every choice he's made, he's made out of fear and self-loathing.

I let him go slightly, unable to stop myself from feeling sorry for him.

"You've always had to struggle," I say, and he seems shocked by my soft tone. "Too bad you've made a lot of bad choices because of it."

"I was set up for them," he insists, and I have to shake him.

"No, you weren't," I yell back, unable to stop the bitter flood of emotions. "My dad didn't have to die because you felt oppressed! If you were sad, if you had a hard life, you should've strived to help others, so they didn't have it so bad—not make others' lives worse!"

His eyes are more sharp now as he looks at me. With my mask on, it's useless for him to try to identify me, but there's something else he seems to be looking for …

"I wondered … if that was really you before," he murmurs.

My hand slips, wondering if he had indeed remembered me.

Before I could grab him again, there are running footsteps that cry out from the pavement below.

"Stop in the name of the law!"

Ben's voice cuts through me the same time his gun fires.

No more than a second later, The Marxman's body goes limp and bloody in my grip.

"No!" I gasp, unable to stop myself from shying away from the blood.

It's too much like how my dad died.

My fingers go numb and The Marxman's body slips away from me.

His body tumbles over the edge of the roof, and he falls.

There's a loud, squishy *splat* on the ground as his body jerks and contorts into an unnatural position.

"What happened, Ben?"

I'm surprised to recognize the voice: Officer Rob Aragon, my dad's one-time friend on the squad. Rob and my dad had worked together on several cases before Dad started working for ELEMENT.

Another man comes up to them, practically screeching with rage. "What happened to these two? I thought you said he wasn't going to hurt them?"

Ben glances up at me.

With one look, I know what he wanted. Ben wanted me to come down and take the fall.

At once, I start to back away, retreating to the shadows.

The autopsy for Kathleen and The Marxman would easily show I didn't deliver the killing shot in either case; I might've roughed up The Marxman, and Kathleen might have been struggling, but I know I'm not to blame for their ultimate deaths.

"Dizchord, come down here!" Ben calls again, and at this, I tuck in my batons even more tightly and head out.

"Time for me to go, I guess," I say. My voice sounds thin and reedy against the night air as I take one last look at the man who'd murdered my father, and the woman who'd been partially responsible for arranging it.

There were more answers yet to find.

Who was this "Selena," and what were her connections?

I have to find her.

And with The Marxman dead, it will only be a little while before another trafficker steps up to try his hand at becoming just as notorious, if not more so.

My heart is beating swiftly as I make my way through the city. My head is full of victory and defeat, joy and sorrow, pride and shame …

Gradually, the warmth of light and life creep back into the sound of the streets; subconsciously, I follow it, and even as I arrive at my church.

The back of St. Elias Church welcomes me home; it seems to stand against the tide of the world, as if to say my suffering is intricately tied to the rest of the world, and the church would remain stoutly against such trouble.

Father Mike knows Dizchord comes at seemingly random hours of the night, eager to confess, to confide—to pray, to seek, to find. The light he leaves on for me is a fatherly blaze of fire, and the Father's forethought makes me wonder all over how Dad has provided for me.

But there's more to do tonight.

I find a small alcove in the sanctuary; it's dark except for the small, electric candles that have been left out, and as I sink into the first pew, my heart slows. My mind feels the first inklings of supernatural peace. My soul brims over with its own broken, beautiful song.

I feel at home.

And so I am.

* ♪ *

It took me years to perfect it, but there's another aspect of my power that I have yet to tell anyone.

I push back my hood; I spy the golden glow in both my palms.

I bow my head, close my eyes, and I pray.

And then I remember Dad, singing with me during church; I remember Dad, playing piano behind me and beside me.

I remember Dad speaking of one who is the Middle C of life.

I think on how Dad's own song is half of my own, and how, using my power, using my gift, I can follow that into the past. "Musical memory" is the best way I can say what it is; "musical time travel" seems misleading in some aspects.

I open my eyes and beside me, looking slightly surprised, is Dad.

It's not my Dad as he is now, but rather as he was; and still is, but in the past.

My power has brought him to me.

"Where am I?" Dad asks, his voice as deep and rich as ever, and I smile.

"Don't you mean "When am I?"" I ask.

He grins back at me, and knowing that his killer has been defeated for the last time, I pull him into a tight hug.

I feel like a child again, in the arms of my father.

"It's okay, son," he says, and I am so thankful all over again for my gift.

After a few moments, I slide back into my seat. "I found The Marxman," I tell him, and he shakes his head.

"Before that, tell me, son … Do you have a girlfriend yet?" He looks so hopeful, I'm torn between rolling my eyes and laughing.

"Dad, come on."

He's told me before not to be afraid to move on with my life, and that even as a dead man, he wanted grandchildren. Sometimes he would look at me and say things like he'd be very proud to have three or more grandchildren, including twins, and I've always just kind of looked at him funny before changing the subject. If Dad pushed, I'd mention I was content to take care of Mom.

It was a bit cruel to say, since watching Mom lose Dad had been one of the worst experiences of my life. Over the years I'd dated here and there, but no one made my heart sing.

"Fine. Then tell me about your mother, Stephen. Is Val still treating her well?"

"Yes." I nod, although I still need to tell him I haven't told her the news about The Marxman yet. Still, I push that concern away.

Ben will probably tell Mom about that himself.

"So she's really doing okay?" Dad presses. He frowns slightly as he watches me, and I nod again.

"Yes," I say, feeling uneasy. I don't really want to talk about this with him. I like Val as my stepfather, and seeing Dad alive makes me feel like I'm betraying both of the good men who have raised me. And it felt even worse because as bad as it had been to lose Dad, things weren't always so bad now. "Val has been good to her. And to me, too. But we don't have to talk about that—"

"No, I like talking about that. It's good to know he's keeping his promises to me. I was pretty tough on him … Hey, by the way, do you remember if you pass your midterm in Mrs. Sanderson's class? You seemed worried about it earlier tonight."

"Mrs. Sanderson?" I let out a quick laugh. "I honestly don't remember. How long ago was her class? Tenth grade?"

"Ah, well, never mind." Dad shrugged. "No harm done, it seems."

"I don't have a lot of good memories with her," I say softly. "I think I would've managed to forget her entirely by now, if not for you."

"Well, you'd be a bit out of sorts in my place, too." Dad puts his arm around my shoulder. "One moment, I'm watching the Falcons game with my fifteen-year-old son, and then the next I'm sitting in church with my twenty-six-year-old son."

"I know it's a shock. But I'm glad you're here."

Since the first time I pulled him out of his time—out of my past and into my future—he's always asked me about Mom first. And then from there, we would move to what date it was, if the Falcons won, if the Braves were still winning, and what bet he could place to get me more money if I needed it for college.

When I was a kid, I used to wonder why Dad would seem to disappear one moment, and then reappear later on; a few times, he would run out, saying he had to go to church at strange times.

Now I know—my future self had called to him and brought Dad's physical reality into his present.

And I also know how Dad managed to amass a growing fortune for me, even though he was technically dead. Thanks to help from Ben and Rob and Sensei Shawn, and even Val, he would organize a way to place bets in his name, and then I'd collect the winnings.

Even though Dad had figured out a way to do it secretly and securely, I'd been more than a little furious when I found out.

Still, Dad rightly pointed out that I could be Dizchord much more easily if I didn't have to worry about money, and for the longest time, I didn't even know I'd been helping him by telling him about the games. He'd further argue with me that I was risking my neck by going after traffickers, same as he'd once done, so him risking his money and "jail time" for going against the IRS was silly.

"Especially if I'm dead," he'd added.

After that, I stopped bringing it up.

"Dad." My voice drops and I turn serious. "I found The Marxman tonight. And he's dead now. He wasn't acting alone, either. Kathleen was working with him."

Dad lets out a sigh. "I see."

I don't know how he remains so calm; I really don't.

When I was a kid, Dad never told me about meeting with my future self. He'd make comments here and there, and there had been plenty of strange things happening when I'd bothered to come out of my cocoon of teenage narcissism. I figure that was why he'd never said anything about his future.

I clench my fists tightly, angry once more.

Dad had known. He'd known he was going to die. He'd known for over a year before it happened, too; he could've avoided it, even … maybe. We're not really sure.

"I've always felt something was off about Kathleen," Dad says a moment later, forcing me back into the present. "She's always played it too safe. And in some ways, ELEMENT did, too."

I think about Kathleen. "She's dead, too. He shot her before he died."

Dad pulls me against him. "It's not your fault, Stephen," he says. "She chose the life she lived."

"Yeah, but she was capable of good, too." I think back to her memories and swallow hard. "I … I think she tried to save me that day. The day you died. We were at the Georgia Dome … "

My voice trails off as I remember Kathleen's memories. She'd said it'd be too much to capture me, that she didn't want to put pressure on "Martin," who I guess was her boyfriend back then, too—The Marxman himself.

At that realization, I shake my head. "But then, who knows if she was really doing me a favor or not? I was the perfect distraction for you, so the girl could get kidnapped."

I look over at Dad. "Maybe if you can find something, that'll help. There are more complications now that The Marxman is dead. I need to find his contact, and I'll need to see to anyone who steps up to try to take his place. And Ben probably thinks I killed Kathleen, too … "

"Well, Ben's a good guy. You'll be able to set him straight," Dad assures me. I notice too much that he refuses to do anything to negate his death, and I leave it at that.

I'd asked him before, and he's insisted he's made peace with his passing.

"I die protecting the people I love, defending the principles I stand for," he'd said. "I could not ask for a better way forward. And I even have the foreknowledge, so I can protect you and provide for you and your mother even after I've been gone."

I flinch even now, thinking of what he'd said. It was so honorably morbid, but so poignantly hopeful. It was something that only could be stated by a man made of honor, who'd lived a righteous life.

And if that was anyone, it was my dad.

My hands glow again, and I know my time is limited.

"I'm only allowed seven minutes," I murmur, more reminding myself than him.

"Well, I'll see if I can do something," Dad says, and I only nod. "Thank you, son. I'll see you again soon."

The unspoken words of love and pride and joy are there, and I try to smile as he disappears.

"Thanks, Dad," I whisper back, as he disappears in a wisp of music and light.

Glancing up at the altar before me, I bow my head in gratefulness. There is silence, but I know there is a heavenly sympathy surrounding me.

Despite the pain of Dad's departure, I know I am not alone. I may have come to church to see Dad, but I still had a Father who was looking after me.

He'd given me a powerful gift, and I would use it honorably and faithfully.

I sit up in the pew, running a hand through my hair before pulling my hood back up.

"Now I just have to figure out what my next steps are going to be."

* ♪ *

And so, the legend of Atlanta's most musically gifted superhero continues! Will Dizchord uncover the truth about The Marxman's criminal ties? Just how much of ELEMENT is involved in all of this? Who can Stephen really trust? Will Stephen ever get a girlfriend? And can the Falcons ever win a Superbowl?

Find out more as Dizchord's adventures continue in the next issue!

* ♪ *

THANK YOU FOR READING!

Please check out https://www.csjohnson.me for
information on the next issue!

DIZCHORD

BEHIND THE SCENES

* ♪ *

come for the story, stay for the surprises …

Dear Reader,

Thank you once more for joining me on a walk through my imagination. I hope you will leave unscathed enough to return in the future, but I also hope your heart has not been left unaffected. One of my greatest joys about being a writer is that I love helping people rediscover their wonder, and if I can have any wish as you read my work, that's what you will find—even if it's just wondering what in the world I was thinking!

* ♪ *

This book is a result of many things, but there's no question that it was divinely inspired. Truly only God could take my growing love of light novels, my contrarian response to social media, growing cultural tokenism, author representation, cancel culture, bad superhero story fatigue, and the increasing resentment toward men in society, and make it into something unique, thoughtful, and hopeful.

* ♪ *

First of all, I would like to say as a Christian, all truth is God's truth, and all stories are God's stories. No matter how terrible it can be, I firmly and fervently believe God can take a story and redeem all the pain it causes. I have seen this in my own life, and I have seen it in others'. That is a big reason I like to write the stories that I do—they are a fantastical reframing of reality, mixed in with supernatural divinity, in hopes that it will rekindle the human soul to reawakening wonder and the God behind it all.

* ♪ *

Of course, with any of my books, there are plenty of silly reasons behind some of more serious ones. *Dizchord* was a bit of a dare for me. In 2022, I saw some of the responses to the latest *Miles Morales* iteration as Thor on social media. As someone who grew up in the Raimi era of *Spider-Man,* and as someone still waiting on *Spider-Man 4 (Spider-Man: No Way Home* doesn't count), I feel a lot of sympathy for Miles. *Into the Spider-Verse* did a fantastic job of introducing him without replacing the OG *Spider-Man* of Peter Parker. However, much like Robin from DC, I feel like Miles ought to eventually be able to grow outside of Peter's long-casting, and well-deserved, shadow. (As a side note, many people who initially responded to Dizchord's lock as "too much like Nightwing's" may have not been far off, but I can assure you, it was a subconscious idea.) The idea of an original black superhero—one who doesn't have "lightning powers," either, according to one of my social media friends—was apparently lost on Current-Day Marvel writers.

I saw this discussion, and I had to say that, as someone who'd never written a comic book before, and as the "whitest-white girl" ever, I could do a better job of it.

So, I decided to make good on my word.

That's the first big truth right there: *Dizchord* is much of a self-dare between me and social media. This is not as big as it seems, since I have written other works—namely *Fatgirl, The Princess and the Peacock, The Divine Space Pirates,* and *Northern Lights, Southern Stars*—largely as a dare before, although there is something much more charged about this one.

Perhaps it is because Dizchord is black, or that it's about human trafficking, or because it's set in my current-home city of Atlanta. Or just perhaps it's because my comic book superhero, even if the comic is my first one, is a character who can easily and proudly stand next to other mainstream superheroes from Marvel, DC, and other indie comics I've loved.

But it's probably the first thing that affects it the most.

I knew going into it that I wanted an authentic character, and while you can ask ten different people on the street and a hundred million or so on social media what it means to be "black," I looked to a lot of literature and history. I've read a lot of classics in my life set in Africa by good writers who captured the heart of the times and gave the rest of the world a glimpse at the souls there. *Things Fall Apart, Cry, The Beloved Country*, and many written folk tales and missionary testimonies and personal tales I've heard all came together to serve as loving points of inspiration. Many African traditions started in oral history, and many still use this to communicate stories, legends, and ideas through their communities; my own black friends and coworkers I've had over the years have been from many different places besides America, including Nigeria, Ethiopia, Kenya, South Africa, and Libya. Many of my black American friends are happy just being from America, even though some don't know for sure where their families originated from. All of Stephen's characteristics (even his name) come from these collections of my friends and the good men in my life. As for myself, I strive to keep my characters honest, but in Stephen's case I especially wanted someone that would be easy for readers to fall in love with.

There is always a bit of fad to write "sympathetic" characters such as Harry Potter or Cinderella (the opposite of Hamilton from my Starlight Chronicles series), people who are down on their luck, and then most people want "relatable" ones, where they're kind of the unoffensive, perceived "normal" ones in a collective cast, like Jim Halpert from *The Office*. But I like to write characters who are honest about who they are, even if they don't realize it. I've found I enjoy reading a character I don't need to relate to, one I don't necessarily like, but one I can understand. Much as Orwell says, I'd rather be understood then loved (largely because to me, loving requires understanding, more often than not). In drawing up Stephen's full character, I had to imagine where his character thread began—and it began in music—and where he was placed, and how he would act in a way that would round out the plot to resonate with both character and theme.

Nothing of this has to do with the color of his skin, but rather his heritage and his heart and his true authentic self. In the event people take notice the color first, I hope they'll also see into his heart and want to stick around for the full series.

There have been a lot—a lot a lot—of discussions about "representation" in media. I have different thoughts about this, as I don't think there's an inherent "right" to it, but I also believe it's a good thing to introduce new voices and new characters. In many ways, the "Charlotte's Web option" must strike again: Just like Wilbur needed Charlotte's children, and her offspring, we need new heroes, and heroes that will speak directly into our own age.

Yet we ought not to discard the old ones. Good writing and good stories, especially about heroes, universally teach its readers about sacrifice, love, and power, and where we resonate and delineate from the characters is where we find ourselves. Old heroes still have plenty to teach us, much like the patriarchs, prophets, poets, and people of the Old Testament. They carried the Law of God forward to Christ, and we find in Christ the Law's fulfillment; and now, having been fulfilled, we need as Christians to be able to carry that saving power forward.

As I see it, heroism is the ultimate form of "university," especially for men: the unity of diversity. We need both unity and diversity if we are to find and bring forth wisdom in our own age. Of course, as a woman, I need it, too; but in light of how anti-men culture seems to have grown, I want to remind men and women that it's not better to be a man or a woman: We need to be *good* men and women, and we are at our best when we work together toward truth, goodness, beauty, and love.

I've seen the lack of this as well as the excess, and I see my own reliance on good men in my daily life. And that's another reason for such a comic: I wanted a good man, with a good father, at the center of things. There is a long history in the debate of "Does art change culture, or does culture change art?" and the answer is obviously, "Yes."

Ultimately, I think our culture, especially with its love of nihilism and postmodernism, needs a change. And it, as it always does, must start with each of us. I've written about this before in Christian Toto's *Hollywood in Toto* site.

It's one of my best articles, if I do say so myself—and I am so pleased with how easy it was to work with Christian and how kind he is, especially for a movie critic!

https://www.hollywoodintoto.com/christian-conservatives-c-s-johnson

Since this is a special novelization of the comic, which you can find on my website, I wanted to add in some important extras for those of you would like to do the same. If God has given you a story to share with the world, I pray you will find a way to make it come into fruition.

If you would like to be a comic book writer, or a novelist (my original gambit), I have some great resources for you to consider in the next few pages, and I'd also like to take the chance to thank (and recommend!) some of the wonderful people who really brought *Dizchord* to life.

FROM BOOKS TO COMICS

* ♪ *

start getting started …

If you want to make your own comic, or you've been curious to see how I got this one made, this section of the book will walk you through my experience. I don't get overly specific, but enough people have asked me about it that I thought I would write it down and charge them for it.

As a side note, I also did a podcast with my friend Laura A. Grace on this topic a few years ago. I was working more with manga and graphic novel ideas at the time, but overall, I'm pleased to say my advice is still evergreen and easily applied to comics.

You can check out the podcast here:

https://www.youtube.com/watch?v=znybnklqjia&pp

I wrote the comic on a bit of a dare, but I have an advantage in that I've been a writer for several years now—over a decade, really—and while it's different from writing a comic, understanding how story elements are supposed to fit together really does help with starting.

So, first step is to have a story. I actually started more with a character—Stephen—but I enjoy more character driven novels (most women do.) What I mean by this is that your main conflict is centered around the character and favors the internal conflict that he or she faces; readers familiar with my work can point to Eleanora from The Order of the Crystal Daggers, Arie from The Divine Space Pirates, Hamilton from The Starlight Chronicles, and Kallie from Fatgirl. There are others, too, but those are the most popular ones. Most of these stories are about living with a new reality, facing fears while finding courage, or falling in love while facing more struggles. When I taught this to my literature classes, I would point to *Finding Nemo* as a great example of a popular movie that was character-driven.

Plot-driven stories are about what happens. *Boom!* *Crash!* *Flash!* The end of the world is nigh, a tragedy is happening, the bad guy is taking over the world, and there's a damsel in distress. Most men like plot-driven stories better. Rose struggles to break her own curse that's been placed upon her in my Once Upon a Princess series; Bjorn has to chase down his brother's beloved, Arja, before she's killed in *The Legend of Eydis*. *Avengers* is the best example I used in citing plot-driven movies, since it has a lot of pre-established characters working together to stop an alien invasion.

I have a lot more to say about character, plot, and story development in general, and if you're interested, you can check it out in my book *Good Writing is Like Good Sex: Sort of Sexy Thoughts on Writing.* You can get the book here:

https://www.books2read.com/goodwritingislikegoodsex

Just like poetry and puns, I enjoy word play a lot. The book is a fun read, and it's nothing graphic if you're unsure of it from the title.

In the previous section, I mentioned a little bit before on how I began to create Stephen's character, building his story around those elements. And then, with the genre conventions and the intended story and adding in some themes I wanted to touch on (grief, loss, power struggles, forgiveness, redemption, and justice, etc.), I put together more of the plot and wrote a very bare outline down.

At the end of all of this, this is what I arrived at: A young man with the ability to hear the music inside each soul goes after the human trafficker who killed his dad.

C'est parfait, really.

Then it's time to get to the more fun and embarrassing part—drawing out your characters.

Or in my case, drawing out your characters badly!

CHARACTER DESIGN

* ♪ *

prepare to laugh …

So once you have your story, with comics, it's time to lose your pride, unless you happen to be a wonderful comic artist yourself.

This is my first drawing of Dizchord:

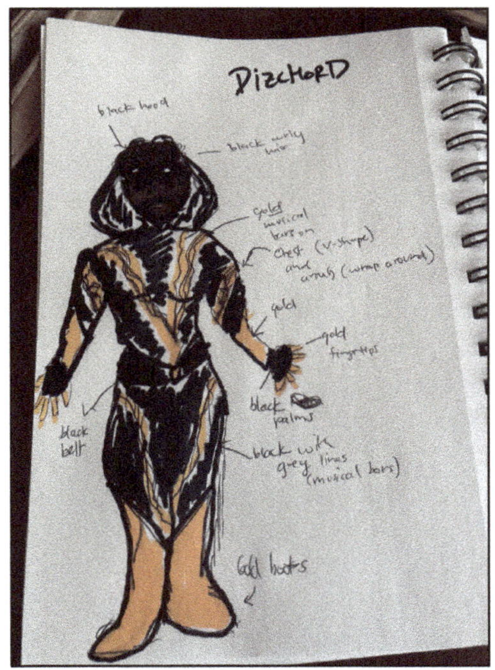

117

Honestly … I've seen worse. And as someone who is *not* a comic artist, most definitely, it was enough that I got it down well enough I could get a good comic artist to draw much better for me.

* ♪ *

Getting a comic artist to work with you is probably the most intimidating part of the comic process—or at least, it was for me.

As a writer, you're alone a lot. And if you're alone enough, I think it's easy to come to prefer it. I don't need to rely on a lot of people to help me creatively to bring forth my stories (emotionally, and editorially, that's when help is desperately needed). Writing a story is just writing down words.

And I can handle words!

Once the words are down, I get a good, trusted editor (I have worked with some really great ones if you need help finding one), and then maybe a beta reader or two, especially if it's in a new genre or an older one I haven't visited in a while. And then I take all this feedback and refine my work, and then get it ready to publish.

But with comics, it's obvious that you need someone who can do comic art.

You want someone who is good at what they do, someone who will be able to do the full run, someone who won't mind working with you as a newbie comic creator (or as someone who may or may not come with a certain reputation on social media, perhaps?

I've seen contracts cancelled because of the usual disagreements.)

And then personally, I wasn't entirely sure I could find someone who would be able to take my drawing of Dizchord and turn it into something that looked like an actual superhero comic character.

As I talk about in the podcast with Laura, I explain about going to places like Upwork or DeviantArt or even Twitter (or "X" now) to see if there's anyone with a style you believe will compliment your story well.

You can even try searching for comic images, which is how I found Light Comic Studio, the team behind *Dizchord*.

Light Comic Studio is particularly appealing to me, since most of my novels have a manga and anime influence to them, and the studio has done both manga and comics, and they work regularly with character design and art.

After talking with them, we negotiated the price for a full, 30-page, full-color comic (know your comic standards!) and a timeline in which I would deliver the script, and they would produce it.

We did exchange a few emails about character design before the script was due, and eventually, my fears of my un-drawable-ness were unfounded, as I got these lovely sketches:

As you can probably tell, they did a much better job than I did!

There were a few rounds where I asked for some minor changes here and there, including things like adding his weapons, and then eventually removing his beard:

DIZCHORD

When we reached the final designs, I finally got the full-color version!

121

122

DIZCHORD

As you can imagine, I felt ecstatic.

I had a great character design, I loved the colors, I loved the look of the character, and my artist team and I were getting along, and we'd settled on the price and timeline.

The worst part was over.

Or so I thought.

SCRIPTING YOUR COMIC

* ♪ *

GET TO WORK!

Here is probably my worst fault as a comic writer right off the bat: I procrastinate terribly. Of course, I am a wife and mother, juggling my family and extended family and all our schedules and activities, along with my own three or four hours of getting to meet with friends or do something on my own, which I desperately need by the time it's available to me. But because I am a good writer, I am also really good at justifying myself when I shouldn't actually do it.

Speaking of which, there is a bigger reason I did procrastinate quite a bit with this project: I didn't know how to write a comic script.

Thankfully, there's another reason for me to love Light Comic Studio: They had worked with several beginners before and sent me some script samples. I was also able to talk to Levi Tonin, who did the artwork for my *The Legend of the Rainbow Unicorn* book.

You can find that amazing one here:

https://amzn.to/45RVUyO

or grab a digital copy on my Ko-Fi shop here:

https://ko-fi.com/s/50dc7a277a

or even splurge and get the audio book here:

https://ko-fi.com/s/f0208b1f00

From Light Comic Studio and Levi, I learned there are three main, basic ways to write a comic script, and I think I chose the one that most resembles a movie script. I took several classes for my MA in screenwriting, but *whispers* college education in the arts can be more of a hinderance than a help.

But I still struggled to write it.

As a practiced writer, I am used to just typing down words as I think them; later, I will go back and change them. And if I have mistakes, I will get one of my fabulous editors to catch them and change them for me. And when I randomly pick up a book four months after I publish it, and I see a typo, I will call my mom and cry and she will tell me everything will be alright.

Writing a script is different from using words. I had to think in pictures, and then write the words that would convey those images to the artist team.

You would think it's not that different from writing; you can probably imagine things just fine from what you're reading here.

For my script, I had to picture how it would look all at once, and then describe it. Usually, as a novelist, it's easier just to focus on the one character and fill in the details as needed. With the visual element, you can't do that. It's the difference between getting a picture on your phone and receiving text messages.

If you still don't think this is different, try taking a picture of a birthday cake and sending it to your favorite texting person. Then text your next-favorite texting person that you're buying a birthday cake, even if it's not your birthday. Repeat this with others

if you'd like, and see how many people arrive at the
same conclusion.
And then maybe you can use some of the birthday
money they send you to buy another one of my
books.

I have described this process before as putting
your pants on backwards—everything is still there, it
feels largely the same, but there's enough about it that
you feel uncomfortable.

There's a bit more added pressure, too, since
when the script is written, and then passed on to
someone else, changes can be expensive and time-
consuming. Throughout the drawing and inking part
of the comic's production, I had one large change to
one panel, and I genuinely feared I'd be booted off
the project for even asking. But Light Comic Studio is
very professional, and very patient with me, and I was
able to get the change made.

Still, I hope they weren't mad at me.

Painstakingly, I did manage to get my script done.
To prove it, as well as show off a bit while I'm
showing you what to do, I've included the first five
pages here, along with their various stages of the
comic's completion.

First, the basic script:

Dizchord, *Atlanta's Guardian Angel of Music*

Page 1 – FIVE PANELS **Reference sheet A

1) Warehouse in Atlanta, after midnight; a large 18-wheeler truck just parked outside; in the left corner, there's a hidden shadowed figure overlooking the scene from on high as two men, human traffickers, discuss the price of their cargo.

A strip of gray-colored music notes <u>pass</u> over the panel; in the shadows, DIZCHORD can hear the music inside the souls of the children being trafficked.

WAREHOUSE DISTRICT IN MIDTOWN, ATLANTA, GA, MIDNIGHT

TRAFFICKER #1:
Come on, all's I'm saying is that we can get a better price—

TRAFFICER #2:
No one breaks their deals with Conductor Marx. He's not known as "The Marxman" for nothing.

2) The two men and their accomplices, another man and a woman are at the back of the truck.

TRAFFICKER #3:
What's this? Someone offered you a better price?

WOMAN TRAFFICKER (TRAFFICKER #4):
I'd hate to tell my boss.

TRAFFICKER #2:
No need to worry him. We got his order right here.

3) Larger panel; the back of the truck is open; in the moonlight, the truck is lined with Hispanic children with tied hands and gags. They look thin, hungry, poor, scared and sad.

4) Warehouse shot; the grey music <u>start</u> to turn gold as the shadowed figure steps forward.

F. X.
Music notes (soothing, lullaby-like tune) ♪ ♪ ♪ ♪ ♪ ♪ (suggest bars for "Moonlight Sonata")

5) In front of the truck; the four villains look around, eyes wide, confused and scared by the music, while the children look a little more scared, hopeful, and curious.

Page 2 -- FOUR PANELS

1) Longer, vertical panel: The shadow (page one, panel 1) moves out into the moonlight

 The shadowed figure is DIZCHORD; still cloaked in black, but music notes on his super suit light up golden as gray music notes are gone and golden mist surrounds him. His eyes are pure gold light as the four human traffickers stare at him.

F. X.
Music notes (jarring – more jazz/swing notes)

2) Woman trafficker pulls out her gun.

WOMAN TRAFFICKER:
Who are you?

3) DIZCHORD's eyes narrow, but he gives no answer as he pulls out his two-part bow staff and puts it together.

4) Larger panel as the men all race forward to attack him; but DIZCHORD is resolved and ready.

intense fighting breaks out; he attacks all the men:

One with punches, one with kicks, and one where he throws TRAFFICKER #3 over his shoulder onto the ground using his staff.

F. X. s
Ouch!
Oof!
Augh!

5) He turns to the woman and knocks the gun out of her hand just after she shoots; the bullet misses him.

WOMAN TRAFFICKER (looking desperate):
You wouldn't hit a woman, would you?

6) He grabs her with one hand and with his other hand, he uses a ball of golden light to put a song of discord into her soul; the glow radiates the power to change the music of the soul, and he sends her spiraling into madness and insanity.

<u>**Page 3 -- FIVE PANELS**</u>

DIZCHORD and the <u>traffickers</u> fight:

1. Dizchord attacks one man (TRAFFICKER #1) with punches

2. Dizchord kicks another man (TRAFFICKER #2) (TRAFFICKER #1's nose is bleeding as he kneels on the ground in pain from the punch)

3. Dizchord throws TRAFFICKER #3 over his shoulder onto the ground using his staff (second man is on the ground, laying on his back, in pain from the kick)

F. X. s
Ouch!
Oof!
Augh!

4. Gunshot rings out from the Woman Trafficker, but Dizchord pulls TRAFFICKER #1 in front of him.

5. As the Woman gasps and TRAFFICKER #1 is bleeding on the ground.

WOMAN TRAFFICKER (looking desperate):
You wouldn't hit a woman, would you?

6) Dizchord frowns; his hands are lit up with golden energy that glows.

<u>**Page 4 -- FIVE PANELS**</u>

1) Woman falls to her knees, weeping and trapped in a nightmare of her own mind as she holds onto her head and screams while the DIZCHORD watches. His power exudes golden music notes with power to change the music of the soul, and he sends her spiraling into madness and insanity.

DIZCHORD
You've collected a lot of regrets since we last met.

WOMAN TRAFFICKER
(crying, faintly glowing gold)
Who are you? What have you done to me?

DIZCHORD

I've only amplified the music of madness and discord that resides inside your soul; you did the rest. But then, I expect that of a dirty cop from ELEMENT. Especially one as dirty as you, *Kathleen.*

2) Smaller panel: Woman trafficker/Kathleen passes out (faints) in shock and pain at hearing her name.

3) Larger Panel: shows all 4 traffickers on the ground, passed out/dead, wounded and bleeding in the moonlight. The three men are bleeding out while Kathleen twitches.

CHILD from the back of the truck.
F. X.
Whimpers

4) Dizchord walks up the ramp into the truck with the children and pulls down his hood.

DIZCORD
Don't be afraid.

F. X.
Music notes, soothing lullaby notes again

5) Dizchord kneels down next to the whimpering child.

I'm here to help you, but if you can wait just a little while longer, you can help others, too. I've been eager to meet *Conductor Marx,* the man who paid these goons to kidnap you and bring you here.

Page 5 -- **FIVE PANELS**

1-2) Dizchord helps untie the kids' binding around their wrists and their gags. Freed children start helping others to get untied.

DIZCHORD
Once I take care of Conductor Marx, federal agents will come. They'll do their best to get you back to your families—or find you new ones.

3) Children look hopeful but still sad.

WHIMPERING CHILD
I want to go home I want my mom!

4) Dizchord pats him on the shoulder comfortingly.

DIZCHORD
What about your dad?

WHIMPERING CHILD
He died shortly after I was born. I've never met him.

5) Dizchord stands up.

DIZCHORD
Maybe you'll meet him again one day. My dad died when I was younger, but I still see him from time to time.

WHIMPERING CHILD
That's impossible!

6) Dizchord looks off into the distance, watching for Conductor Marx.

DIZCHORD
Sometimes the impossible becomes the inevitable ...

Next, using this, my artist team sent me the initial drawing and inking stages:

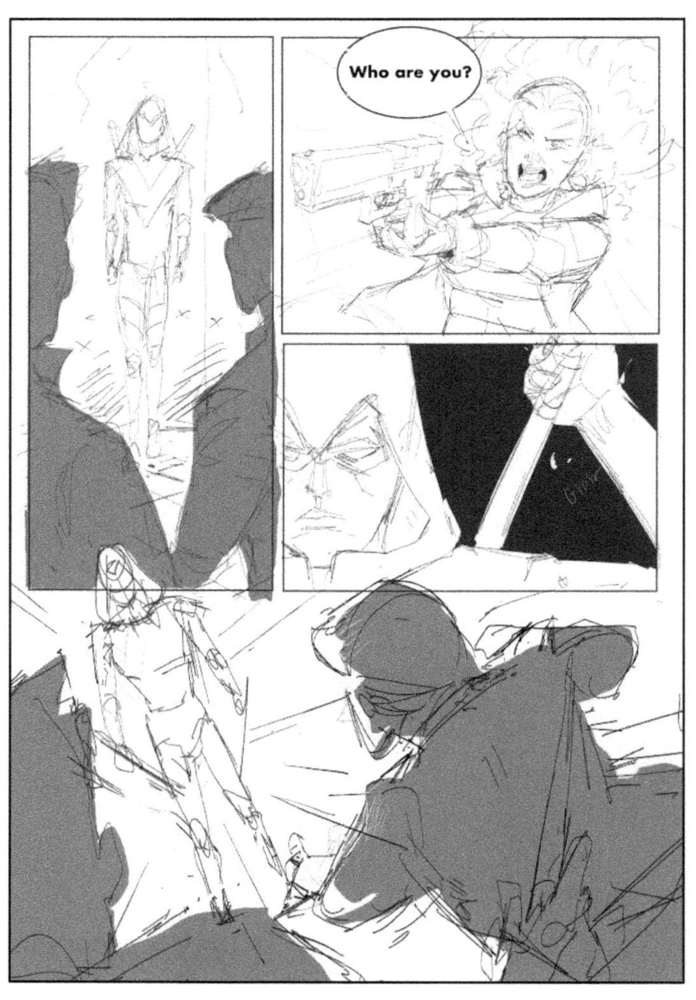

Who are you?

OUCH
OOF!
BANG
BANG
AUGH
YOU WOULDN'T HURT
A WOMAN,
WOULD YOU?
DROP
Fall

What have you done to me?
I've only amplified the music of madness and discord that resides inside your soul; you did the rest —
and you would have done worse to others if I hadn't shown up to stop you.
But then, I expect that of a dirty cop from ELEMENT. Especially one as dirty as you, Kathleen.
He knows me?
He knows me!
Don't be afraid.
I'm here to help you, but if you can wait just a little while longer, you can help others, too.
I've been eager to meet Conductor Marx, the man who paid these goons to kidnap you and bring you here.

Once I take care of Conductor Marx, federal agents will come. They'll do their best to get you back to your families
—or find you new ones.
What about your dad?
I want to go home. I want my mom! I miss her!
He died shortly after I was born. I've never met him.
Maybe you'll meet him again one day. My dad died when I was younger, but I still see him from time to time.
That's impossible!
Sometimes the impossible becomes the inevitable ...

And then finally, the coloring:

DIZCHORD

WACK!
UOF!
WHAMMM!
GRAB!
BLAM! BLAM! BLAM!
KONG!
DROP!
YOU WOULDN'T HURT A WOMAN, WOULD YOU?

What have you done to me?
I'VE ONLY AMPLIFIED THE MUSIC OF MADNESS AND DISCORD THAT RESIDES INSIDE YOUR SOUL; YOU DID THE REST —
AND YOU WOULD HAVE DONE WORSE TO OTHERS IF I HADN'T SHOWN UP TO STOP YOU.
BUT THEN, I EXPECT THAT OF A DIRTY COP FROM ELEMENT. ESPECIALLY ONE AS DIRTY AS YOU, KATHLEEN.
HE KNOWS ME?
HE KNOWS ME!
DON'T BE AFRAID.
I'M HERE TO HELP YOU, BUT IF YOU CAN WAIT JUST A LITTLE WHILE LONGER, YOU CAN HELP OTHERS, TOO.
I'VE BEEN EAGER TO MEET CONDUCTOR MARX, THE MAN WHO PAID THESE GOONS TO KIDNAP YOU AND BRING YOU HERE.

ONCE I TAKE CARE OF CONDUCTOR MARX, FEDERAL AGENTS WILL COME. THEY'LL DO THEIR BEST TO GET YOU BACK TO YOUR FAMILIES
—OR FIND YOU NEW ONES.
I WANT TO GO HOME. I WANT MY MOM!
WHAT ABOUT YOUR DAD?
HE DIED SHORTLY AFTER I WAS BORN. I'VE NEVER MET HIM.
MAYBE YOU'LL MEET HIM AGAIN ONE DAY. MY DAD DIED WHEN I WAS YOUNGER, BUT I STILL SEE HIM FROM TIME TO TIME.
THAT'S IMPOSSIBLE!
SOMETIMES THE IMPOSSIBLE BECOMES THE INEVITABLE ...

As you can see, it's a wonderfully lovely and fascinating process!

In between all these stages, I had my editor check over each page for typos—because there is always at least one that gets through—and I requested feedback from some of my comic friends I'd met over the years.

Overall, I think *Dizchord #1* turned out great, especially for a first official comic. I've had a lot more feedback since my various campaigns went live, and I'll be making some changes for Issues 2-5.

As a side note to this, given how long the production of this comic took, I recommend making sure you've got the full script written out as much as possible.

I am currently learning this the hard way, as I'm working on the outlines and scripts for Issues 3-5 (#2 is finished!). While I have the story planned and I know the ending—perhaps my greatest piece of advice, after all the rest of it—as of writing this, I still have yet to finish writing all of it down and sending it along the editor-to-publishing pipeline.

Before I go any further, I want to highlight a very important aspect of writing—something that you absolutely will need.

DIZCHORD

144

SUPPORT TEAM

* ♪ *

you absolutely will need this!

When you try something new, it's exciting—and also scary.

As a former teacher, I've seen enough to believe (or not enough to disbelieve) that anyone can reasonably and truly learn anything he or she truly desires to learn. And that "anyone" includes you. If you set your mind to it, anything within reason is possible; sometimes, even things are possible without reason.

And if there's anything I've learned through my years of pain, suffering, and agonizing stress of being a teacher, it's that a *good* teacher will hold your hand through the whole process.

That is mostly figurative, but it can be literal, too. And contrary to a lot of power fantasies, it hints at the other cursed blessing of human nature: We learn from each other, and we depend on each other, and we need each other.

You need a support team.

In the age of the internet, this seems easy; fans and friends and people of peripheral interests can easily find you if you desire to make yourself known.

But the truth is also "easy come, easy go," and it can be very simple to cut people out of your life that came into it simply, too.

As a comic writer and a writer in general, and even as a person in general, find someone who can be happy for you without hating you, someone who can cheer you on even if they're sad, and someone who will hold your hand in a death grip if you try to wriggle your way out of it.

Writing a story is like having a baby. Everything comes together in the dark spaces inside you, you get mood swings, you're tired and restless and full of energy but terribly distracted. You need people who will give you space and give you grace.

Not everyone has that, and some people can still work. I deeply admire them, because I'm not one of those people, and the good Lord knows I need my team.

When it comes to my books, I have so many people to thank on a regular basis I have to be creative in saying thanks or they'd be bored to death by now, pummeled by my pathetic "thank you" murmurings. At least changing it up enough makes it harder to string me up on a murder charge.

There are just so many people I need to thank, too.

I have my fabulous editors—Cathy, Crystal, Faith, and Jennifer—and my cover designers, Les and Olivia and Amy. I have a lot of good go-to contractors for audio books, too, like Alio, Jennifer, and Will. I have my small but powerful group of my (Almost) Famous Readers, run by the incomparable Malissa, and in that group, I have my comic-art/manga-loving friends Jacob, Jon, Laura, and Timothy.

Thanks to my comic endeavors, I have met more people that have helped me so much along the way, like Lan, Levi, Theo, and Spencer—all of whom did some incredible artwork for me for *Dizchord*.

And when I started my promotional tours, I was able to get so much help from people like Christian, CN, Luke, Nick, Paul, Pedro, Peter, RJ, and Society so many more souls who were willing to spread the word about my comic.

And then just after God, the best support I get is from my husband.

One of the best things about being as happily married as I am is that Husband is here for me. And when my crises come, he has such a good, wise sense of humor.

Ah, how can I not love him all the more for it, too?

* ♪ *

I am an indie publisher largely because I like doing things by myself. But the truth is, that's an illusion.

In writing books or comics, or creating anything else, you will need help.

Start collecting a reliable, trustworthy set of people. This may be a book, or it may be some friends, or it might be an online group. Either and any way you do it, just make sure to get it done!

GETTING STARTED!

* ♪ *

stuff I use to write, print, publish, & more …

WRITING

Can't replicate myself, but get a good editor, read a lot of good books (read an older one, and then a newer one to help get a feel for the genres' evolution—Nora Roberts in her early days is different from Nora Roberts in her current days … and I said "different," not "bad" … and not "better," either), have fun, and get people who will give you honest feedback on it.

You don't need a "Yes!" man; you need with the ruthlessness of a "The Devil Wears Prada" boss *and* the bubbliness of a "Bring It On" cheerleading squad.

EDITING

I have a little extra help with editing thanks to ProWritingAid.

https://prowritingaid.com/

149

I'm not an affiliate but I like it. Get a promo code or wait for a sale. It's good but don't pay more than you have to.

DESIGN WORK

There's a lot of ambiguity that can go into art—or what passes for art these days—but I recommend Canva to take care of most of it.

I have the paid version right now for the CMKY coloring for my comics; I think it makes it richer and more lively, and ultimately more fun. But the free version is the best way to go for 99% of my other work.

https://www.canva.com/

It's also a very easy platform to learn how to use, since YouTube or Rumble or Odyssey can help you if you get stuck.

PUBLISHING

For my comic floppy, I had a lot of good advice from Luke Stone (@LukeStoneStudio on Twitter). He gave me a good template for comic books—one of my biggest, most embarrassing "newbie" moments with my comic was getting it made in a 6 x 9 size, whereas comics are 6.5 x 10.25). I was able to get it fixed and reprinted easily thanks to PrintingCenterUSA.

https://refer.printingcenterusa.com/g8xxec72

This is where I'm good with my comics, but I'd also like to give you other resources for books in general.

For hardbacks with dust jacket covers, I've used Lulu and mostly liked it. They've gotten better since they've added in a Canva extension to help you adjust your book covers as needed. They make you order a proof copy and get it delivered before you can sell to market, and that's my only complaint about it. I don't get refunds for books I order that I end up wanting to change.

Still, I've never had a serious issue, and the dust covers are nice.

https://www.lulu.com/

I use Ingramspark for most of my physical paperback books and some of my hardbacks, although it tends to be my hardcase books and not the jacketed ones.

151

Ingramspark has stopped charging you for book setup fees so it's gotten much better in the last year. They do take more of a percentage out of your sales, but it's generally worth it. If you sell direct, you can order them from your own account at a reduced price and that's easy enough to do; the printing turnaround is not as quick as Amazon though, so make sure you've timed your estimated deliveries as needed.

Some other authors I know don't like it, so your best bet is to get a copy of your book printed out first and see what it's like. If you like it, great! If you don't, they've been good about refunds.

https://www.ingramspark.com/

Ingramspark has a good distribution center, but I like using them along with Amazon's KDP platform best.

https://www.kdp.amazon.com

It's free to sign up and it's Amazon, so you'll get your books in front of readers.

The nice thing with Amazon is that the ebook options are all there, too.

For all the non-Amazon ebook platforms, I use Draft2Digital. You can upload everything there and your book will get on multiple platforms. You can sign up for free here:

https://www.draft2digital.com/writercsjohnson

After they combined with Smashwords last year, the only mainstream holdout to Draft2Digital is Google Play:

https://play.google.com/books/publish/u/0/

Of course, you can add your book to your own site as well, and because there are a myriad of options available for that customization, I'll skip my own methods and tell you to do your research and decide what's best for your needs and resources.

FUNDING

This is not hard at all for me. If you're making a book, try Kickstarter.

https://www.kickstarter.com/

If you're making a comic though, go to FundMyComic.

https://www.fundmycomic.com

FundMyComic is the super-IQ brainchild of Luke Stone, and it's great. It's personalized for visual media like comics and graphic novels, and I loved getting my money on time, with only the 2% processing fees, and there was always help when I needed it.

FUN EXTRAS!

* ♪ *

you won't want to miss this!

Writing a comic can be daunting, but it is full of fun! And here I get to share some of those fun things with you!

ANIMATION

More people love to see trailers when they do comics for crowdfunding campaigns. With *Dizchord #1* Pedro Caicedo (@Nguila on Twitter) did a great job on one for me!

https://www.youtube.com/watch?v=HqhjWpsn4x8

ARTWORK

Theo, who designed this book's cover, was one of the first YouTubers I met who seemed genuinely interested in my comic, and I was very happy to work with him. He's done some great work for some of my

155

other upcoming stories, too, so I am especially pleased to recommend him.

He does commissions if you want some great, special artwork and his family is making a whole universe of superheroes.

You can find him @Crea_TV_ on Twitter.

I mentioned Luke Stone before (@LukeStoneStudio) and I also recommend him for comic book art and commissions. I am especially pleased to announce here in this book he'll be doing the variant cover for *Dizchord #2*! And I am so excited!

Spencer Baculi (@KabutoRiderMav on Twitter) is also a great person to work with! He's done some things for my Fatgirl superhero satire series, and he's

DIZCHORD

also drawn me some great shots of Dizchord, including this line art:

Levi Tonin is a great artist who's done some previous work with me, and I asked him to do a variant cover for *Dizchord*. While I didn't get the milestone for that unlocked, I still really love the picture. It's my background picture on my phone screen currently.

DIZCHORD

MARKETING

Honestly, there's nothing I hate more about being a writer than marketing. I'm an introvert that has something to say, so I hate trying to pitch my ideas to people; I just want them to read it and like it, and you'd think putting it all together and getting it ready for other people to enjoy it would be enough.
Nope!
So these are some of my best recommendations for people to check out and query:

Peter Pischke of *CultureScape*
@HappyWarriorP on Twitter

Peter does a lot of interviews with people at the forefront of culture war issues and interests. He's had novelists from companies like Baen, comic book artists like Ethan Van Sciver, and critics like Christian Toto and Chris Gore.

Speaking of Christian Toto …

Christian Toto of *Hollywood in Toto*
@HollywoodinToto on Twitter

Film critic and cultural commentator Christian Toto is happy to talk about new projects that are upcoming and speak into modern-day areas of interest. He's approved some of my guest posts and has been a great voice in culture from the more right-wing, conservative perspective.

For a more libertarian center take, check out the next guy!

Leon Idol of *Words of Paradise*
@BoltTheWord on Twitter

Leon does a few weekly shows and has a channel talking over news. He likes to feature a variety of creators about gaming, sci-fi and fantasy, and comics.

The Common Nerd
@CommonNerd1791 on Twitter

CN does a few shows a week also talking about culture, comics, Christianity, and more. He's a big family man and seems to be a gatekeeper for the future as he sifts through new creative content and current events. He has several returning guests and cohosts that keep things fun, light, and also a little dark at times.

Nickweiser
@Nickweiser on Twitter

CN and Nick are great friends, so it's cool to see how they bounce off each other. Most of their topics overlap in some way, but it's been great chatting about comics with both of them.

Jacob Airey of *StudioJakeMedia*
@realjacobairey on Twitter

159

A media junkie, Jacob always has something to say about the state of media, especially when it comes to comics and anime. He has a lot of great articles on books, manga, movies, and more on his site. I've had a few livestreams with him and we just love talking to each other.

As a side note: Jacob was also one of the first people I really befriended on Twitter and he's like a brother to me. So send him an email and see if he's up for reading and reviewing your work.

Katie Roome of *Periapsis Press*
@RedHedgeDragon on Twitter

I've never seen Katie turn down an interesting book, and certainly not one of mine. She does reviews on her site Periapsis Press and she and her husband David, who is also an author himself, do many things to help promote other indie and "Iron Age" creators. Katie's website has a contact form where you can reach out to her about your book or comic.

Paul Hair, writer for *Bounding into Comics*
@PaulHair on Gab

As a writer himself, Paul knows what to look for in a good book. Paul writes articles on people and projects of interest for Bounding into Comics, my current favorite comic book and culture news place on the internet.

Paul did a very nice feature on *Dizchord* for me when I was about to launch my first campaign on Kickstarter.

<u>Jon Del Arroz of *The Dankstream*</u>
@delarroz on Twitter

Jon has been a successful and prolific indie comic writer for many years now. He's also a novelist and he has a channel where he and his guests can talk about some industry news and upcoming projects. Jon is great to reach out to if you need encouragement and he's got a lot of information up about how to write a good comic. He and S. A. Rivera of *Literature Devil* helped provide a lot of my initial research into writing comics, and I am so grateful for that.

<u>SPECIAL MUSIC</u>

<u>Diggz</u>
@DiggzDaProphecy on Twitter

When I wanted to write a superhero with musical empathetic powers, I listened to a lot of music. I live in a very musical city, and the Southeast/South is full of musical memories. Diggz read my comic and produced a great song out of it.

https://www.youtube.com/watch?v=4swPajbb4bQ

I'm putting this in here to give you ideas, although if you ask him to write you a song, you might be fortunate like I was.

Diggz is a skillful music composer and mixer, and he really loves anime and comics. I really consider it an act of God that we met on @BoltTheWord's podcast.

OTHER TOPICS

That's really about all I can think of right now. There's a lot of trial and error when you start out on a new project like this.

The best advice I can give you, having done it now for ten years—even throughout all the shifting landscapes of the internet and modern-day culture concerns—is to keep doing it. G. K. Chesterton once said that anything worth doing was worth doing poorly, and you never know what kind of greatness you can offer the world until you free it from your heart and soul.

That is something worth doing, even if it's only for yourself, or just something you and God can share.

<u>SIGNING OFF!</u>

* ♪ *

that's all for now …

There's always a lot out there to do and learn, and I hope if you've read through to this part, you've found some good thoughts and ideas to get you started on a new adventure.

Thank you once more for joining me during this book. Each book is a part of me, and a part of my heart, and I am very happy when I get a part of the reader's heart in return.

That's all for now! Time for me to get back to work on my next story.

Until We Meet Again,

CJ

C. S. Johnson

DIZCHORD

* ♪ *

C. S. Johnson is an award-winning, genre-hopping author of science fiction and fantasy adventures such as *The Starlight Chronicles, The Order of the Crystal Daggers, The Divine Space Pirates*, and more. With a gift for sarcasm and an apologetic heart, she currently lives in Atlanta with her family. Find out more at https://www.csjohnson.me.